Meet Pastor Goodenough

A Humorous Look at Life in the Parish

Lyle L. Luchterhand

MANKATO, MINNESOTA
INTO YOUR HANDS LLC
2016

Into Your Hands LLC
Mankato, Minnesota
www.intoyourhandsllc.com

Meet Pastor Goodenough: A Humorous Look at Life in the Parish, by Lyle L. Luchterhand.

This is a work of fiction. Names, characters, businesses, places, events, incidents, etc. are either the products of the author's imagination or used in a fictitious manner. Any resemblance to actual persons, living or dead, or actual events, is purely coincidental.

ISBN–10: 0–9857543–5–4

ISBN–13: 978–0–9857543–5–8

Library of Congress Subject Headings
Christianity—Fiction
Clergy—Fiction
Wit and Humor—Religious Aspects—Christianity

First printing, June 2016.

Contents

Introduction

What happens when a less than perfect young pastor is assigned to an even more imperfect congregation? What chance does a puppy have swimming in a tank of piranhas? The young pastor survives—with a little help from his wife and friends!

Meet Pastor Goodenough shines the spotlight of humor on some of the difficult situations in which ministers find themselves. It tells how Willie B. Goodenough is introduced to All Sports Lutheran Church, his morbidly curious congregation in Cadaver, Wisconsin; how he suffers through a wedding he must perform for a motorcycle mama; and, how a building project is approved only because of the timely assistance of his two pet cats. This book presents characters who carry their weaknesses to an extreme.

While it may be easy to imagine some of the antics described as actually happening, we want the reader to know that the characters described are entirely fictional and any resemblance to actual persons is purely accidental.

My forty-six years as a Lutheran minister have taught me that people are often inordinately curious about those in the ministry. Many categorize the clergy as hopelessly helpless and love to criticize them. The pastor, on the other hand, desperately wants to be loved. *Meet Pastor Goodenough* depicts in a humorously exaggerated way the tension that may arise between a pastor and his flock. It also reminds us that both pastors and their church members are always in need of improvement—indeed, in need of forgiveness, which of course is the whole point of the church. Hopefully, the lessons included in each chapter will assist with some of that improvement and leave pastors and laity alike smiling to realize how forgiving God must be to put up with all of us. If that happens, this little book of humor has served its purpose.

Special thanks to my dear wife Jean and to my friend Dr. Michael Dietz for their encouragement and suggestions.

Lyle L. Luchterhand

Chapter One:
The New Pastor

For four years Willie had suffered the slings and arrows of outrageous seminary professors. Those four long years seemed like an endless Wisconsin winter. Willie had burned midnight oil, immersed in theological training, and without regard for his financial future, accumulated staggering amounts of debt. And all that time he had no idea where on Planet Earth the Lord would send him. But soon he would know! Today was Call Day at the seminary, the day he and his classmates would be assigned a church.

At the breakfast table that day there was one more earnest discussion between Willie, the graduate, and Missy, his wife of two years. "I'm so worried, Willie. I'm so worried. What if we never see our families again? What if we don't like the place where we're going or the people we're sent to serve?"

Full of optimism and faith, Willie replied, "Honey, the Lord knows what He's doing. He'll find a good place for us. Besides, it's our job to love our people. And since the people we serve will be good Christian people, they'll love us too."

A few hours later, sitting in the seminary chapel, Willie and Missy were still waiting to hear where they were going. Finally the announcement came: "Willie B. Goodenough, All Sports Lutheran Church, Cadaver, Wisconsin!" So that's where they were going! All Sports Lutheran Church, Cadaver, Wisconsin!

But what kind of name was "All Sports"? Most churches had religious names like Beautiful Savior or Prince of Peace. Why would a church call itself "All Sports"? And where was Cadaver, Wisconsin? They'd never heard of it! Didn't Cadaver mean "dead body"? If there was a restaurant in Cadaver, did anyone dare order meat off the menu? Whose liver did they serve with their "blue plate special"?

After their arrival in Cadaver they learned why the church was named All Sports. Some forty years earlier, a man named Hans Kantschrift served as the church secretary. People wrongly assumed that Hans could read and write, simply because his father had been a schoolteacher. But Hans couldn't read, and he didn't know one end of a pencil from the other. When he filed the incorporation papers, he had the name "All Sports" filled in instead of "All Saints." But looking back, everyone agreed that this so-called "mistake" was the perfect example of accidental genius, because none of the people at All Sports were ever interested in being saints. Sports, on the other hand, were important to them.

To say that the new pastor and his wife caused a stir when they arrived in Cadaver would be an understatement. People were obsessed with curiosity. Everyone was deeply envious of those who lived next door to the new pastor. People next door could just look out of their windows and spy on the newcomers. Everyone else had to find some other way. People drove their cars down the street past the parsonage. People rode their bikes past the parsonage. People walked their dogs past the parsonage. They pushed their babies in strollers past the parsonage. They borrowed other people's dogs and babies just so they could walk by, all of them pretending not to look. People hid behind bushes with binoculars, pretending not to look.

One of the trustees of the church, Mr. Ralph Grossbeak, even climbed into the church's bell tower to see what he could see. He couldn't see much. But Ralph leaned out too far, fell eighty feet and became Pastor Goodenough's first burial at All Sports. That's how Pastor Goodenough met his fishing buddy Freddie Plantemdeep, who was part owner of Slabum and Plantemdeep, an enterprising little funeral home in the neighboring town of Comatosa.

But even Ralph Grossbeak's falling out of the bell tower didn't put a stop to the endless parade of cars, trucks, vans, semis, farm tractors, garden tractors, motorcycles, horse-drawn carriages, bikes, baby buggies, baby strollers, walkers, and joggers that kept parading past the parsonage, pretending not to look. Soon even nature joined in. All the birds, rabbits and squirrels in Cadaver gathered in the pastor's yard, hoping to get a glimpse of the new pastor or his wife, all of them pretending not to look. When it rained, thousands of raindrops dripped down the windows of the parsonage, pretending not to look.

People were running out of disguises to wear as they paraded past the parsonage, pretending not to look. They were putting too many miles on their cars going past the parsonage, pretending not to look. They were wearing out too much shoe leather. Not to mention what they were doing to the street! In some places the asphalt on the street had been worn down to the thickness of an eggshell.

There were two things that finally brought people to their senses and ended the parade of cars, trucks, vans, baby strollers, walkers, and joggers. One was when Izzie Inkblot crashed his crop dusting plane in the back yard of the parsonage while flying too low and pretending not to look. The other was when Farmer Joe Rubberneck drove his tractor down the street and dropped his plow without realizing it, because he was so busy pretending not to look.

Everyone said those were the straightest six furrows Joe Rubberneck had ever plowed, but they didn't do much for the street. When Joe realized what he'd done, he quickly sent his son over with a disk and seeder and seeded it all down in winter wheat, hoping no one would notice. But people did notice. And when Joe plowed the street, the town council decided enough was enough. They blocked off the street and refused to open it until a year later.

But by then nobody cared. People had discovered that it was difficult to find something to criticize about the new pastor and his wife by just going past the parsonage, pretending not to look. They were finding other ways to criticize. They diligently compared Pastor Goodenough to all the other pastors they had ever known—none of *them* very well loved either—and began to find all kinds of differences between the new pastor and all the others they had known. Everything they discovered became proof that there was something wrong with the new pastor.

Their last minister, a man named Gottlieb Doolittle, was quite old when he died in office. Who could blame the people of All Sports for thinking that all ministers should be at least fifty years old? It was obvious that the new minister was way too young.

And who could forget the first worship service Pastor Goodenough conducted? The old pastor wore a plain black gown. When you looked up at the dark altar area, it was hard to see where he was standing or where his voice was coming from. But when the new pastor came out of the sacristy that first time, he came out like an angel of light, wearing a shimmering white gown that practically glowed in the dark. And instead of saying, "Don't be afraid," as angels were supposed to say with their very first words, this angel said, "Hi, I'm your new pastor, Willie B. Goodenough." When people heard that, they didn't know if they should stand up, sit down, or go to the hospital to be treated for shock.

Pastor Doolittle had a voice as deep as a bullfrog's. He had a slow and methodical way of speaking. He took great pride in not being interesting. It was easy to catch up on sleep during his sermons. The new pastor's voice was an octave higher. He actually moved in the pulpit. He told stories and used illustrations. He spoke with emphasis. When he preached, it was as if the congregation had passed around a bottle of No-doze. Obviously, there was something wrong with the new minister.

One woman, appropriately named Miss Kitty Litter, knew she wasn't a very good judge of character. But she didn't want to be left out. She too wanted to pass judgment on the new minister. So she decided that when the new minister came over, if her cat liked him, she would, too. If her cat didn't like him, she could tell the whole world that the new minister was somehow defective and couldn't be trusted. As sure as God made little green apples, when Pastor Goodenough visited, her cat Stinky Boy was shy and aloof around the new stranger. So Miss Kitty Litter quickly got the word out to the community. There was indeed something wrong with the new minister.

There also was some criticism saved for the minister's wife, Missy Goodenough. Like her husband, she was too young—certainly too young to be married. She was only twenty-five. Her dresses were too short. She used too much make-up. She was too pretty for a minister's wife. None of the women in the Ladies Aid were less than sixty years of age. None of them wore anything smaller than a size 20-1/2. Missy wore a petite size 8. How would she possibly fit in?

Pastor Goodenough and his wife Missy didn't know that people were putting them under such a high-powered microscope. They didn't know that all the words they spoke were repeated over and over again until they weren't the same words anymore. Outwardly, the people of All Sports were friendly and kind. Every night in their prayers Pastor and Missy Goodenough thanked God for bringing them to this wonderful place and sending them to serve such wonderful people. *They didn't realize that even in the church some people may only pretend to be your friends so they can be more effective as your enemies. Would the Goodenoughs ever fit in at All Sports? Would All Sports ever learn to accommodate them?*

Chapter Two:
Good Ole Betty May

It was Sunday morning at All Sports Lutheran Church. Betty May Sparks had arrived early to hand out bulletins, catch all the gossip and, though she would never admit it, she also came early so she could secretly inspect the janitor's work. Betty's husband Ralph was about to retire from the mill. That janitor's job would provide just the right amount of money Ralph and Betty needed to supplement their social security and pension.

From the moment Betty May joined All Sports Lutheran some thirty-one years before, she had accepted the awesome responsibility of keeping things going there at All Sports. Not that she ever wanted to have an office in the Ladies Aid, or head up the funeral meal committee. That anybody could do! No, Betty May Sparks held things together at All Sports in a different way. She was quality control. She was prosecuting attorney, judge, jury and executioner at All Sports. If the janitor forgot to replace a burned-out light bulb, if somebody in the choir sang bass when he should have sung tenor, if the minister paused too long between announcements at the end of the service, Betty May Sparks took it upon herself to make appropriate suggestions.

And it wasn't just *what* she said. It was *how* she said it. Who could forget the day she waved that spider web in front of the poor janitor's face? How she ever got that spider web out from under the organ bench intact without breaking a strand—that was something only Betty May could do. She extracted that whole spider web, complete with the empty shells of two centipedes, one millipede, and some new type of bug that all the entomologists at the University still haven't identified.

It was a once-in-a-lifetime discovery, for which Betty May got her picture in the local newspaper along with a nice write-up. It was on the religion page, smack dab alongside an article on the new Catholic church going up across the street from All Sports Lutheran.

That's what made all the Lutherans squirm, when Our Lady of Only Holy Desires Catholic Church decided to build a new church. The rivalry that existed between those two flocks had flourished for decades. Every Sunday morning the Lutherans took all the good parking spots in front of the Catholic Church, and the Catholics parked in front of the Lutheran Church. It was the only time all week they acknowledged one another. They had to say "Hi!" "How are you?" "Nice weather today, eh?" as they crossed the street and met one another face to face.

The rivalry was unrelenting. When the Lutherans' well went dry, the Catholics decided they'd better drill a new well, too, even though they didn't really need one. When the Catholics had their annual polka mass and steer roast, the Lutherans made sure they garnered more profit from their annual bazaar and beer tent. When Father Janski got a new car, the Lutherans slipped Pastor Goodenough a little extra money with the understanding that he'd get a new car just a little better than Father Janski's. It was a proud moment for all the Lutherans at All Sports that day last April when Pastor Goodenough parked his new Buick Park Avenue in front of the Catholic Church opposite Father Janski's Mercury Sable, which was parked in front of the Lutheran Church.

But to the pastor's and the father's dismay, this rivalry also included which church could pay their man of the cloth the smallest salary. "You pay Father Janski how little?", the Lutherans would say. "We get our minister for $2,000 *less*!" Both churches would have gladly paid their minister nothing at all just to have the bragging rights, but nobody could figure out how to swing it.

Lately, the Lutherans had been on a roll in their rivalry with the Catholics. They were winning every round in this game of ecclesiastical one-up-man-ship until this new Catholic church, this $1,500,000 gauntlet, had been thrown down in their face. This would have been hard to top. Thank God for Betty May. It was a stroke of genius that Betty May found that new bug that nobody could identify. This was something the Catholics were unable to match.

That's what made Betty May's presence there at All Sports something that all the little folks could tolerate. Betty May was always so critical of everybody. She had such an inflated sense of her own importance. *But now she really was important.* In one fell swoop Betty May had nullified whatever effect the new Catholic church would have on the Lutheran-Catholic rivalry in town. One magnificent, Lutheran bug had once and for all leveled the playing field no matter what the Catholics did. Bring on a strand of hair from the Virgin Mary. Bring on a holy mouse trapped at the Vatican. Bring on the Shroud of Turin or the Holy Grail. As long as the Lutherans had their bug, which they were justly proud of, and which Pastor Goodenough had wisely baptized, instructed, and confirmed Lutheran the day it was discovered—as long as they had that Lutheran bug, they were more than a step ahead of the Catholics.

It was always a treat for the folks at All Sports Lutheran when Betty May handed out bulletins. You heard things you otherwise would never have known. "You know that young Susie Q. Weber who married young Johnny Blair last month? Well, she's been at her mother's house for the last four days, ever since Johnny implied that her cookin' wasn't as good as his mother's. And young Tony Dufus took one of those identical Franklin twins to the dance last Friday and went home with the wrong one. How was he to know?"

"And, get this!" Betty May said. "Last night Pastor and Missy Goodenough had their first big quarrel, and it was a doozie! First they argued about how you're supposed to replace a toilet paper roll. Then Missy got on Pastor's case about why he always squeezes the toothpaste tube in the middle and why he won't pick up his dirty socks off the floor. Then Missy wanted to know why Pastor was always putting empty cartons in the refrigerator. Can you imagine? Yesterday Missy found an empty milk jug, an empty orange juice bottle, an empty egg carton, an empty pickle jar, and an empty butter box all in the refrigerator! Shouldn't empty bottles and boxes be thrown in the trash? I don't know how Missy can live with that man!" With her verdict spoken, Judge Betty May Sparks was on her way to tell someone else all that she knew.

Everybody who entered the church that day found out immediately about Pastor and Missy Goodenough's first big argument. And it was during those last five minutes before the service started, when everybody sits in his or her pew alone with his God, those last solemn moments when everybody is supposed to be deep in prayer, getting mind and body ready for worship, those last solemn moments when the organ is playing softly—that's when people were thinking about how to replace a toilet paper roll, and where to squeeze a toothpaste tube, and whether they had picked up their dirty socks off the floor. When Pastor Goodenough walked down the side aisle toward the front to get ready for the service, during those last solemn moments when they were alone with their God, those last solemn moments when everybody was supposed to be deep in prayer, getting mind and body ready for worship, those last solemn moments when the organ was playing softly, everybody was thinking about Pastor Goodenough and his absent-minded habit of putting empty cartons back in the refrigerator.

The ringing of the church bell startled everyone out of their pious, religious thoughts. And then Pastor Goodenough walked out in all his glory ... his long white gown, his flowing green stole, his wonderfully white clerical collar. He welcomed everyone to this solemn yet joyous service and then announced that the sermon that day would be dedicated to the subject of "Gossip."

At that moment two teenage girls started to giggle up in the balcony. One thing led to another, and soon the whole congregation was roaring with laughter until the tears were rolling down people's cheeks and people were patting one another on the back and trying vainly to catch their breath. Laughter, deep-bellied, uproarious laughter rolled from one end of that church to another, until the people simply couldn't laugh anymore. That was the day everybody in that congregation became friends. All the tension that had built up, all the wrongs that had been done through the years, suddenly melted away and everybody did indeed love one another. Only Pastor and Missy Goodenough remained in the dark about what had really happened that day, what the laughter was all about.

But that was the kind of effect that Betty May Sparks had on All Sports Lutheran Church. Bugs were discovered that people had never seen before. People knew amazing things they otherwise would never have known. And yet everybody knew that Betty May talked too much. Betty May knew too much. Just step out of line once and not just Betty May but the whole world would know what you had done.

Compared to Betty May, her husband Ralph Sparks was a saint. How he could stand being married to that woman, nobody knew. Some people thought Ralph was driving on a flat. His elevator didn't go all the way to the top. His driveway didn't go all the way to the street. The light was on, but there was nobody home. There were too many birds on Ralph's antenna. He didn't have both oars in the water. He was three bricks short of a load. He was runnin' on empty. Well, whatever the problem was with Ralph, there had to be a special place in heaven for anybody who lived with Betty May Sparks. *And surely, even the Lord's patience was being tested.*

Chapter Three:
The Perfect Christmas Eve

Snow was falling at All Sports Lutheran Church. Huge flakes were floating in the air like little balls of cotton. They danced from side to side, landing softly on the sidewalk. People were walking to church in a winter wonderland. It would be a perfect Christmas Eve.

Outside the church some teens from the Youth Group were dressed as shepherds and wise men. Four of Farmer Blanton's sheep, two of his lambs, and his two pet goats, Pete and Repeat, were scampering among a dozen bales of hay and straw. People were pleasantly surprised to see the shepherds, wise men, and animals. "Just like that first Christmas," everybody said, as they carefully stepped over the sheep droppings that littered the sidewalk.

In the Fellowship Hall the Sunday school staff was getting the children ready for the Christmas Eve Service. There were the usual last minute emergencies. Three of the five eighth graders who had lead parts in the service had called at the last minute to say they wouldn't be there. Little Nancy Sugarplum had to go to her grandmother's house for the annual Christmas gift opening, and her parents had decided to skip church and go to Grandmother's house early. One of the Appleblossom twins had the flu, and their mother decided that if one of the twins couldn't go to the Christmas Service, it wouldn't be fair to let the other one go either.

For the staff this meant some hurried substitutions. Pastor Goodenough, who was 6'3", volunteered to be Tiny Tim. Mrs. Octuplets, who was the mother of eight, offered to be the Virgin Mary, and good old roly-poly Farmer Blanton was told that he was Santa Claus.

The children always behaved reasonably well on Christmas Eve. It was the parents you worried about. For most other services people sat in the back, plastered on the back wall like flies on a screen door, anxious to get out. But for the Children's Service people fought for a front row seat. It wasn't unusual to see people pushing in on one side of a front pew and forcing people off the pew on the other side. And if the person pushing in on one end had eaten a little too much butter in his lifetime, it might be two for one sliding off on the other end.

Even during the service the grownups were noisy and disrespectful. People with cameras kept popping up and down like popcorn, taking flash pictures. Some were walking around with video cameras, talking loudly into their cameras. Those were things you expected at the Children's Christmas Eve Service. Through the years it had become more of a circus than a service.

The crowd finally hushed as the children marched in, led by Pastor Goodenough, who was now dressed as Tiny Tim, and by Farmer Blanton, dressed as Santa Claus. The children knew their parts and sang with enthusiasm. Everything went well until it was time for Tiny Tim to speak his lines. *But Tiny Tim wasn't there.* Pastor Goodenough had retreated to the sacristy, where he was sitting in the bathroom, dealing with the Appleblossom flu.

Thank goodness Farmer Blanton was a no-nonsense, take-charge kind of person. He didn't know where Pastor Goodenough had gone or why he was gone. He just knew somebody had to be Tiny Tim. And since he had all the parts of the Christmas play right there on the script handed him just moments before, he played both parts. He got down on his knees facing in one direction to speak Tiny Tim's lines. Then he got up, walked a couple of steps, turned and faced the other direction whenever he was Santa Claus. He played both parts brilliantly—and completely unrehearsed. His booming voice could be heard throughout the church.

To this day nobody knows how Farmer Blanton's pet goats, Pete and Repeat, got into the church. Speculation was they heard Farmer Blanton's voice and thought he was calling them. One of the shepherds or wise men probably opened the door and the goats scampered in before anybody could stop them. Nobody wants to believe that the Youth Group did something like that on purpose. Of course, to this day, no one in the Youth Group will even admit to being at the church that night.

But with all the commotion that accompanied the Children's Service, most people didn't even notice the goats at first—not until Pete Blanton was standing on the altar chewing on the candles and Repeat Blanton had climbed into the pulpit and was tearing pages out of the Bible. That's when Farmer Blanton saw them and let out a string of words that mothers don't ever want their children to hear, certainly not on Christmas Eve. Mothers rushed to the front to cover their children's ears. Then they hurried their children out the door—but not before every one of them gave Farmer Blanton a generous piece of their mind!

Inside the church, the chase was on as roly-poly Farmer Blanton tried to catch his goats. He chased them around the altar, through the poinsettias, around the Christmas tree, through the pulpit, up the aisle, and to the balcony. The surefooted goats seemed to be laughing as they sprinted along the balcony rail with Farmer Blanton in hot pursuit. While they sprinted, he just inched along, clinging in terror to the balcony rail. He was deathly afraid of heights. By this time he was also out of breath, panting, wheezing, and clutching his heart. But anger and frustration drove him on. He was determined to catch his goats.

Once again they went around the altar, through the poinsettias, around the Christmas tree, through the pulpit, up the aisle and to the balcony sprinting and inching along the balcony rail. All the while Farmer Blanton was panting and wheezing and clutching his heart. It was during the three Blantons' third trip around the Christmas tree that Pete Blanton hooked a string of lights with his horns and was momentarily stuck in the tree. Fortunately for him, Repeat Blanton was right behind him, thrust his horns into Pete's posterior and got him moving again before Farmer Blanton got there. The tree was already leaning when Farmer Blanton hit it. Like timber falling in the forest, it groaned and slowly crashed on the church floor.

When the Christmas tree went down, Farmer Blanton finally stopped. He realized there was too much damage being done. Besides, he couldn't get any air. His heart was pounding out of his chest. Pete and Repeat were too fast, yes much too quick, and they weren't afraid of heights like he was. So he sat down in the front row, which was empty now, in one of those choice seats that dozens of grown people had fought over just minutes before. He rested for a while, surveying the damage done to the church. Then he reached into his pocket for a hanky to mop his brow, and he felt the carrots in his pocket. He pulled out a huge carrot and, without thinking, held it high in the air. *And suddenly the chase was on again.* This time the goats were chasing Farmer Blanton to get his carrots—around the altar, through the poinsettias, around the fallen Christmas tree, through the pulpit, up the aisle, and to the balcony, inching and sprinting. But then, in a stroke of genius, Farmer Blanton ran out the door, and the goats followed.

At that very moment Pastor Goodenough left the bathroom and stepped out into the altar area. Now it was his turn to survey all the damage, *and he had no idea what had caused it.* The candles on the altar were chewed down to the nubs. The pulpit Bible lay in shreds on the floor. Most of the poinsettias were flattened. The church was empty. There was no one sitting in the pews, not even in the front pew, which moments before had been fought over. The Christmas tree had been tipped over. Worst of all, the offering plates were standing empty on the altar, which meant that he might not be paid at the end of the month. What had happened? Who had destroyed this beautiful church?

Pastor Goodenough studied the tragic scene for some time. Then, thoroughly bewildered, he locked the church doors and trudged home to his loving wife Missy, who quickly filled him in as to what had happened. And while they were sitting there by the family Christmas tree, watching the fire in the fireplace, Pastor Goodenough poured out his heart: "Honey, I didn't know what was happening over there. I had nothing to do with it. But you know, somehow the good people of All Sports will blame me for all this. They always do."

Missy Goodenough listened sympathetically to her husband's lament. Then she gently took his hand and said, "You know, Honey, things aren't really so bad. Do you realize this is the earliest you've ever been home on Christmas Eve? So far this Christmas Eve no one has called and threatened suicide if you didn't come over and counsel them out of it. Nobody has called to complain that their candy bag had only one candy bar instead of two. And so far no one has interrupted our Christmas Eve and demanded that you go over to the church and help them find a lost necklace or camera. *Honey, do you realize that finally, this Christmas Eve, it's just you and me and baby-to-be?*"

That was the first time Pastor Goodenough learned that he was about to experience the awesome privilege and responsibility of being a father. *Suddenly Willie realized how quickly and how easily God can bring something good out of chaos.* It was the perfect Christmas Eve indeed.

Chapter Four:
The New Baby

The news that Missy Goodenough was expecting a baby hit the people of All Sports like a lit match in a dynamite patch. The Catholics in town were understandably angry, because another little Lutheran was going to be born. But *their* irritation was nothing compared to the uproar this caused among the members of All Sports Lutheran Church.

Troubling questions were raised. *Did the pastor and his wife ask the congregation if they could do this?* Could this poor, struggling congregation of less than 400 people afford another mouth to feed? How many children would the pastor and his wife have? Would they have so many that their two-bedroom parsonage wouldn't be big enough? Would they be like Pastor and Mrs. Prolific in the neighboring town of Comatosa who had twenty-one children before they finally quit?

What kind of parents would they be? They had no experience at it! No one had even seen Missy Goodenough hold a baby in her arms. Why would the Lord entrust a precious, tender, innocent child to people who had absolutely no experience taking care of such a child?

When the little monster becomes a toddler, will he mark up the walls of the parsonage with his crayons? Would the Goodenoughs get a cat or dog at the little devil's urging? Would there be pet mice, pet rats, pet gerbils, hamsters, guinea pigs, rabbits, pot-bellied pigs, ferrets, fish, canaries, parrots, turtles, snakes, lizards, or even pet rocks? *Would anyone be safe going into that house*? How much damage would be done before the house would collapse? Somebody better set some limits! The chairman of the congregation, the Council, the Elders, yes, *somebody* better have a talk with the pastor before this childbearing thing gets out of hand!

That was the congregation's first reaction to the wonderful news that Missy Goodenough was expecting a baby. Thankfully, everybody settled down a bit before anything rash was done. But the news of the coming baby was the choice topic of conversation every time ladies of the congregation got together. They asked one another, "When is the baby due? Are we sure there aren't twins or triplets in there? What does Betty May say? Who's the doctor? Can we find out anything from him?"

Thankfully, some of the people in the congregation began to think a little more positively about the coming baby. Pressure was put on the Ladies Aid to have a baby shower for Missy. Isn't that what other congregations did when their pastor's wife was expecting her first baby? Soon all the women of the congregation were buzzing with excitement over the prospect of having a baby shower.

The shower was finally scheduled for 1:30 p.m. on the first Thursday of May. That meant that none of the working women of the congregation would be able to attend. But the hands of the Ladies Aid officers were tied. The Ladies Aid *always* met in the afternoon of the first Thursday of the month. Nothing could be done to change that.

There was some disappointment when it was learned that Missy Goodenough herself wouldn't be able to attend because of her job, but that soon faded when the Ladies Aid officers announced that they would open Missy's gifts in her absence so everyone could see what she got. The officers would then present the gifts to Missy privately.

It all worked out wonderfully. The officers of the Ladies Aid were the center of attention as they opened Missy's gifts and thanked everyone for participating. They enjoyed a great moment in the sun in front of all their admiring Ladies Aid members. And later, when they presented the gifts to Missy, they claimed exclusive praise and gratitude from her.

There was one mistake made by the Ladies Aid secretary, Miss Ima Airhead. Ima lost the list of who had given what. Consequently, Missy was unable to thank anyone individually. She could only send a general thank-you card to the Ladies Aid organization for its generosity. Some of the ladies found it hard to forgive Missy for that, but in the end cooler heads prevailed.

Missy felt the first labor pains at exactly 3:01 a.m. on Sunday, June 29. She woke her husband at exactly 4:01 a.m. Two minutes later, as soon as he could get his pants on and find his car keys, Willie made a first hair-raising, wheel-squealing, rubber-burning trip to the hospital. At 4:08 a.m. he returned home to pick up Missy. Then he made a second hair-raising, wheel-squealing, rubber-burning trip to the hospital, this time with everybody on board.

By 6:01 a.m. Willie said good-bye to his wife and trudged out to his car to go home. Unfortunately, it was Sunday morning. He wanted to stay to comfort his wife in her peril, but he had to conduct services that morning or there would be consequences.

Soon after Willie left the hospital, the members of All Sports, alerted by Betty May, began to arrive at the hospital. They filled the parking lot with their cars. They filled the two small waiting rooms in the hospital. They filled the hallways of the hospital. They paced back and forth in the waiting rooms and hallways like expectant fathers and grandmothers. *Every one of them had secretly smuggled in a gift for the baby, which they intended to present to the child immediately after its birth.* In their pockets and duffel bags, they were hiding pets they no longer wanted. There were pet mice, pet rats, pet gerbils, hamsters, guinea pigs, rabbits, pot-bellied pigs, ferrets, fish, canaries, parrots, turtles, snakes, lizards, and even pet rocks—all the animals, birds, lizards and snakes they had once hoped would never see the inside of the parsonage.

At exactly 8:01 a.m., when the worship service began, there were only four people in church: the pastor, the organist, and two visitors. Everyone else was at the hospital anxiously awaiting the moment they could give away their unwanted pets. Pastor Goodenough thought about slipping away to the hospital. He desperately wanted to be with his wife in her time of peril, but he had to conduct the service because of the two visitors. As he patiently chatted with the visitors after the service, he was at a loss to explain where his congregation was. He only knew where he wanted to be: at the hospital!

Finally the moment came when he could rip off his gown, jump in his car and make a third hair-raising, wheel-squealing, rubber-burning trip to the hospital. *But when he got to the hospital, there was no place to park!* He drove around and around the hospital until he finally found a parking place three blocks away. He parked and then ran to the hospital entrance, only to be barred from entering by a fire marshal. No additional people could be admitted to the hospital, because the building had reached its capacity.

Willie was beside himself with anxiety and disappointment.

Somehow he had to get into the hospital. He looked up toward the second floor, where he had left his dear wife in her peril. There were all the missing members of All Sports Lutheran Church looking out of the windows! They were all at the hospital to witness the birth of his baby! "How wonderful!" Willie thought. *"But if only he could get one of them to leave the hospital so he could enter!"*

Then the Lord Himself took matters into his hands. All the animals, birds, lizards and snakes people brought began to get restless. They began to escape from the pockets and duffel bags where they were hidden. The snakes began to chase the mice and rats. The larger animals began to chase the smaller animals. The smaller animals ran up the men's trousers and the women's skirts, trying to escape. The men were dancing, trying to shake the rats and gerbils out of their pant-legs. The women were screaming, trying to dislodge the lizards and pet rocks out of their skirts.

Finally, the whole menagerie of dancing, screaming people fled down the stairs, out of the hospital and into the parking lot, taking all the animals, birds, lizards and snakes with them and trampling the fire marshal along the way. Knowing there was room for him now, Willie dashed into the hospital. He ran up to the second floor into his wife's delivery room, just in time to witness the birth of his son.

Three days later, after Willie and Missy brought little Kenny B. Goodenough home, they were sitting in front of the fireplace reminiscing. Willie said, "Missy, isn't it wonderful that all the members of All Sports were at the hospital wanting to share in our blessed event?"

Missy replied, "Yes, Willie, that really was sweet of them. But I would rather have had *you* there. It was like a circus with them. They even asked me if I wanted to buy into their pool predicting the exact moment little Kenny B. would be born. And they made all kinds of suggestions regarding what we should name the baby. They wanted us to name our baby Agnes if it was a girl and Ernie if it was a boy. Honey, the names they picked for our baby were disgusting!"

"Haven't you noticed, Willie? The people of All Sports are constantly interfering in our lives. Remember the silly rules and regulations they made when we moved into the parsonage? We couldn't hang pictures, because that would put holes in the wall. We had to keep our thermostat at 58 degrees in the winter to save money, but they kept their thermostats at 68. They wouldn't let us plant an apple tree in the back yard. And now they wanted to name our baby! *I know you're the minister and I'm the minister's wife and we live in their house, but we're people too, aren't we, Willie? When are they going to treat us like people, Willie? When are they going to treat us like people?"*

Chapter Five:
The Rapture

It was the Eighth Church-Skippin' Sunday after Pentecost at All Sports Lutheran Church. John Smiley was serving as head usher for the first time—and there he was, trying to read that page of ushering instructions while Betty May Sparks informed him that someone had planted a fingerprint on one of the windows in the church entryway. What was John going to do about it? A couple of weeds had come up during the night in the flowerbed. Wasn't that something the head usher should take care of?

John Smiley knew he had to get away from Betty May's mind-numbing, spell-binding oratory. He had to ring the church bell a half hour before the service. That was job number one on the usher list. But in his rush to get away, in the confusion of all those unfamiliar ushering instructions, and in his frustration, *realizing that Betty May was now following him,* talking first about the dirty window, then about the weeds in the flower bed—in all that confusion John Smiley did the unthinkable. *He pulled the wrong bell rope. He pulled the funeral bell rope!* He pulled it slowly and firmly, just as the other rope was supposed to be pulled. He pulled it twelve times, according to the ushering instructions, once for each of the twelve apostles. He pulled for Andrew and Peter, for James and John. Then he ran out of names for the apostles and assigned the rest of them a number. He pulled until he had pulled for twelve.

When the people living near All Sports heard the funeral bell, they all rushed to their phones to find out who died. Which twelve-year-old in the congregation had died? Was it little Caitlyn Chicktobe, who had just had the misfortune of turning twelve? Or was it young John Smiley, Jr., who was nearly thirteen and had almost escaped the grave danger of being twelve?

When all those folks living in the same neighborhood dialed their phones at the very same moment, the effect was like the disaster at the men's dorm at the university a couple of months before. Every toilet was flushed at exactly the same time in every bathroom on all six floors. Water mains and sewer pipes burst all around and under that dormitory. Floods of water, irresistible, relentless, cascading floods of water carried books, lamps, and small refrigerators full of beer out of first floor windows. Even the Dean's puppy, which had been missing for three days, was suddenly flushed out of a window.

That was the kind of calamity that took place when all the people living around All Sports Lutheran Church dialed their telephones all at once. Telephone lines melted. Relay stations faltered, then fizzled. No one could get through.

It was an overflow attendance at All Sports that morning. With the phone lines down, people had to go to church to find out who had died. Of course, they found out that nobody had died. John Smiley had simply rung the wrong bell.

Now please understand that once people entered the church that morning, they had to stay for services. You couldn't leave church once the elders had seen that you were in town. You weren't sick. You didn't have company. You had no excuse for not being there, because, well, you were there. At least there was one consolation for those who were there by mistake, and that was that none of their twelve-year-olds had died.

Apparently, Pastor Goodenough was the only one in town who didn't know that the wrong bell had been rung at All Sports that morning. While the bell was being rung, Pastor Goodenough was in the sacristy putting the finishing touches on his sermon. He was so engrossed in what he was doing, he never noticed John Smiley's mistake! The first indication he had that something strange was going on was the large crowd gathering in the church entryway. There'd be a record attendance that day!

But how could that be? It was summer! People usually skipped church in the summer! Suddenly, Pastor Goodenough remembered that the previous Sunday he had preached about "Death & Hell." *That's it!*

That had to be it! Finally he had found a topic that had shaken the pillars of apathy there at All Sports. Of course, that was it! It must have been his vivid and unforgettable descriptions of hell! Just last Sunday he had described the agonies of hell as they had never been described before, not even in the Bible. He had described how people would squirm in the fires of hell, just like ants trapped in a campfire, like little birds who couldn't fly caught in a forest fire, like missionaries boiled in a kettle by cannibals. In Pastor Goodenough's descriptions of hell more worms had squirmed, more flies had been fried, more toads had been torched, more ants had been blanched than in a 1930s Grade B movie.

That must have been the reason! That's why the whole town had turned out for services on that summer Sunday! Like a crazy, mad scientist, Pastor Goodenough had stumbled on the magic elixir, the secret formula, the perfect solution. He had finally put the fear of God into them. And why stop now? That's why Pastor Goodenough stayed in the sacristy that morning and never found out why so many people were there. He was too busy revising his sermon, turning up the heat and adding more descriptions of hell.

It all worked out better than Pastor Goodenough had hoped. Just when he climbed into the pulpit, one of those strong summer thunderstorms arrived. And only the crassest unbelievers in town still insist that what happened next was only coincidence. Every time Pastor Goodenough said the word "hell," it thundered. Every time a worm squirmed or a fly was fried or an ant was blanched it thundered. The Lord Himself was providing the special effects. Pastor Goodenough never had so much fun preaching a sermon. There was standing room only, even in the balcony. People scared to death, dreading the next clap of thunder, wiping their brows with their handkerchiefs, fanning themselves with their Sunday bulletins, hoping against hope that somehow, someway they might get home safely from church. Not one of them had ever been so afraid in his whole life.

Faster and faster Pastor Goodenough spoke, and more and more frequently it thundered until finally Pastor Goodenough realized he couldn't keep up. So, in a desperate act of self-preservation, hoping to catch his breath, he said, "Amen!" Everyone was relieved.

Then the offering was collected—a bountiful offering that kept flowing over the edges of the offering plates. That tremendous crowd with standing room only, even in the balcony, kept filling offering plates until all their money was gone. They were so happy that all of them, especially their twelve-year-olds, were still alive. It took four ushers to bring the offering plates to the altar that Sunday.

Then Pastor Goodenough turned and faced the altar for that long prayer that follows the sermon. And suddenly, the thunder stopped, and all was strangely quiet. That's when John Smiley looked out of the window and saw that the sky was black. Not just plain black, but a purple, yellow, and orange black. The whole sky was swirling. A tornado was on the way!

None of John Smiley's ushering instructions had prepared him for this. He wanted to yell, "Tornado coming! Get into the basement! Run for your lives!" But as head usher one of his duties was to preserve the sanctity and serenity of the service. How could he interrupt the pastor as he prayed at the altar? So while the pastor prayed that long prayer, facing the altar, thanking God for manifold blessings, asking God for manifold favors, John Smiley began quietly to usher everybody into the basement.

"Dear Lord," Pastor Goodenough droned on and on, "grant that all of us assembled here may escape the sudden destruction and punishment we deserve. Grant us good weather, good health and long life. Help us lead lives without fear, confident of your continual blessing. And finally, when our last hour shall come, bring us to heaven to be with you." Then, just before he was about to say, "Amen," he began again. He chuckled a little under his breath as he said: "And dear Lord, help us escape the agonies of hell, where worms squirm, and flies are fried, and toads are torched, and ants are blanched." But no one heard those last words, because by this time everyone had fled to the basement.

Finally Pastor Goodenough finished his prayer, and he turned from the altar to give the benediction—only to find that there was no one there! That tremendous crowd with standing room only, even in the balcony, was gone. Immediately, Pastor Goodenough, who in the past had always rejected the idea of the Rapture, realized that it must be the Rapture! The Lord had returned to take all the righteous to heaven and He had left the wicked behind! And of all the people in the congregation only he was left!

Now it was Pastor Goodenough's turn to be afraid. He fell on his knees, facing the altar in utter terror. He cried out: "Please, Lord, take me, too! Don't leave me here alone! Take *me*, Lord. Take *me!*" That's when the tornado lifted the steeple off the church and carried it into Farmer Blanton's hayfield. The noise was so deafening and the knowledge that only he was left behind so frightening that Pastor Goodenough fled. He fled to the basement. There he was joyfully reunited with his people. There he discovered that all of them were safe! Only their twelve-year-old steeple would have to be replaced.

That day Willie became a lot more aware of something that everyone else had long ago realized: he, too, was a sinner, just like everybody else.

Chapter Six:
Attitude Adjustment

Worship services were over at All Sports Lutheran Church. The Church Council was gathering in the soundproof Mother's Room for its monthly business meeting. Pastor Goodenough counted heads, discovered a quorum, and opened the meeting with prayer.

"Hope this'll be a short meeting, Pastor. The football game starts at noon." It wasn't unusual for Lenny Quickstep to request a short meeting. Lenny Quickstep hated church meetings, unless, of course, they were accompanied by a free chicken dinner. In that case, Lenny always ate his chicken quickly and left before business was discussed. There was always some emergency at home or elsewhere.

Lenny Quickstep's claim to fame at All Sports Lutheran was the twenty-six years he served as chairman of its church council, but especially the first year he served. Most council meetings weren't even held that year, and those that were probably shouldn't have been. There wasn't enough work done to make them worthwhile. There was no long-range planning done that year. No short-range planning. No widows and orphans provided for.

Lenny Quickstep was especially proud of one Monday night meeting that lasted only three minutes and twenty-seven seconds. After a short prayer by the pastor, Lenny called the meeting to order, the secretary read the minutes, the treasurer passed out his report, and the meeting was adjourned. Three minutes and twenty-seven seconds! Thanks to Lenny, everyone got home in time to watch the kick-off on Monday Night Football with beer and popcorn in hand.

Even though he was chairman, Lenny wasn't concerned about getting a lot of work done at the church. *The less the Church Council did, the less opportunity people had to complain.* That was the philosophy Lenny lived by.

Lenny Quickstep wasn't the only blockhead serving as an officer at All Sports Lutheran Church. Erv Klipstein had been the treasurer for thirty years. During all that time Erv was so tight with the congregation's checkbook that he refused to pay many of the legitimate bills that had to be paid. Erv wasn't at all intimidated by threatening letters from bill collectors. Even when the utility companies shut off telephone, electric, and gas service to the church, Erv would not relent. He'd pay those bills if and when he felt like it. It gave Erv a tremendous feeling of power to have control over that checkbook, the kind of power and authority his wife never allowed him to have with their checkbook at home!

Every time utility service was cut off at All Sports, people knew that Erv was having another one of his battles with the congregation's creditors. For the uninitiated, for those who didn't understand what was going on, the folks at All Sports just said that Erv suffered from a severe case of checkbook writer's cramp. Nobody knew how to explain it and nobody could defend it.

Erv never realized that he was destroying All Sport's reputation in the community when he refused to pay the bills. He didn't think about that. He just wanted to keep all that money in one sacred pile for himself. Once, in an unguarded moment, Erv admitted that his ultimate goal was a zero budget. *The less money spent and the less work done for the Lord, the better.* That was the philosophy Erv Klipstein lived by. It was a philosophy his buddy Lenny Quickstep agreed with completely.

The people at All Sports knew that Lenny and Erv needed an attitude adjustment. Lord knows, they had tried to change the way things were done. More than once they had tried to remove Lenny and Erv from office. But every time an attempt was made to elect someone else, word would leak out to Lenny and Erv. Warned in a timely fashion, they would invite all the riff-raff of the congregation to come to the annual meeting, all the scofflaws to whom they were conveniently related.

The voter turnout would be tremendous. People who had quit the church or even died long ago would come in to vote for Lenny and Erv. Whether reinstated or resurrected or brought in as cardboard cutouts, they were there to vote. They voted early and often, just as Mayor Daley's Democrats were rumored to do in Chicago. When push came to shove, the forty voters of All Sports would always cast the majority of their eighty votes for Lenny and Erv. It appeared that the two rascals would hold office forever.

A loud knock at the door startled that fine group assembled in the soundproof Mother's Room, interrupting their meeting. Pastor Goodenough went to the door, looked out, and with obvious excitement said to the Council, "Come here, fellas. You have to see this!" They looked out, and there was an angry mob sitting in the church pews, chanting, "Justice, justice, we want justice!" There were police patrolling the aisles to make sure the mob stayed seated. The front of the church was set up as a courtroom with a portable judge's bench. *And on the judge's bench, in all her finery, and with a half-dozen television cameras following her every move, was none other than Judge Judy!*

Instinctively, Lenny and Erv knew the jig was up, the cheese was slipping off the cracker, their saw was biting air, the sand was draining from their hourglass, their goose was being cooked. The cork on their champagne bottle had popped, but the wrong people were drinking the champagne! It was time to get while the getting was good! They dashed for the window to escape. But when they opened the window, they found the building surrounded by the National Guard. There were army tanks and armored personnel carriers all around the building. There was even a contingent from the Ku Klux Klan burning crosses on the church lawn, one for each of them. Escape was impossible.

Before anyone could say the words "attitude adjustment," Lenny and Erv found themselves on trial before Judge Judy. An endless parade of plaintiffs presented detailed, written evidence of all that Lenny and Erv had done or failed to do during the previous twenty-six and thirty years, respectively. There were representatives from the utility companies. There was the fifteen-year-old boy who tried to make money for college by mowing the lawn for All Sports—who had mowed that lawn now for more than two years running—and still wasn't paid. There was the man who always dug the graves in the cemetery, who was never paid. There were two roofers, three bricklayers, four piano tuners, and 103 visiting clergy, none of them ever paid. There was the organ man, the furnace man, the Culligan man, the Orkin man, the Chemlawn man, the Roto-rooter man, and the Schwan ice cream man, all of them presenting evidence, all of them with families, all of them showing pictures of their starving families and demanding to be paid.

For a couple of hooligans who hated long church meetings this was the longest church meeting Lenny and Erv had ever attended. For a couple of "good ole boys" who loved a pat on the back and shunned personal criticism, this was the most thorough critique they had ever received. For a couple of insensitive bullies who loved to threaten and trash talk other people, this was more trash talk than they had ever wanted, and it was being shoved into *their* ears. It went in loud and clear. It went in upright, upside down, and sideways. It just kept coming. And there was no free chicken dinner served with it!

Finally, after several hours of directing that choir of angry plaintiffs, Judge Judy retired from the bench for a few moments. Then she came back and pronounced judgment on Lenny and Erv. Lenny lost his office for complicity with skullduggery. Erv was sentenced to pay the bills he had refused to pay all those years, all 249 bills for a grand total of $184,388.03. Fortunately, he had the money, because he had actually squirreled away more than $185,000 in the church's name, money that no one besides Lenny and Erv knew the church had. But worst of all, now Erv had to hand over the church's checkbook! *His power, that awesome, frightening power to say, "No!" and to hold innocent, harmless and starving people hostage—all that power was gone!*

Late that night after the trial, Pastor Goodenough was reminiscing with his wife, Missy. They were sitting in front of the fireplace, winding down after the excitement of the day. Willie asked her all the usual things: how the sermon went that day, how the choir sounded. As they talked, someone called and reported that Lenny and Erv were packing up to leave town! Twenty-six years, yes, thirty years of suffering for that poor congregation were finally over!

In that quiet moment sitting before the fireplace Pastor Goodenough said to Missy, "You know, Honey, I don't understand how Judge Judy got involved in all this. And who gathered all those people together to finally get the goods on Lenny and Erv? And who thought of bringing in the police so things didn't get out of hand? And who got the governor to call up the National Guard with the tanks and armored personnel carriers so Lenny and Erv couldn't get away?"

Missy Goodenough smiled at her husband's bewilderment. Then she slowly got up, went over to her husband, lovingly patted him on the shoulder, and said, *"You know, Honey, sometimes we pastors' wives are good for something. We try to get things done."*

That day Missy taught Willie some of the fine points of people management and problem solving. And thanks to Missy Goodenough, the people at All Sports Lutheran Church also learned a valuable lesson. *They were reminded that while the wheels of God's justice may grind slowly, they grind exceedingly fine.*

Chapter Seven:
The Wedding

Sweetie Pie Sparks was getting married on Saturday. For Sweetie Pie and her parents, Ralph and Betty Sparks, it was the wedding of the century. For Pastor Goodenough, it meant that Hell Week had arrived at All Sports Lutheran Church.

Sweetie Pie's real name was Martha, but nobody called her that anymore. The last poor devil who called her Martha got a finger in the eye. Sweetie Pie was the nickname she received as a baby, because she was always smiling and happy and everybody loved her. Unfortunately, things took a dramatic turn when Sweetie Pie was in third grade. That's when Sweetie Pie changed from being sweet to sour, from angelic to demonic.

It all started when big Bully Boy Peterson pulled little Sweetie Pie's pigtails at school one day. Sweetie Pie decked him with a left hook and a right cross, knocking him out cold. When Bully Boy finally got up, Sweetie Pie knocked him down again. And from that time on, every fight on the playground found Sweetie Pie in the middle, kicking, scratching, clawing, hair pulling, ear biting, eye gouging, karate chopping, and punching. There were knees to the groin, elbows to the stomach, and fists to the Adam's apple. Sweetie Pie perfected the leg sweep, the atomic drop, the pile driver, the back-breaker, the body-slam, and the chokehold.

Nobody was safe. The bigger they were, the harder they fell. Sweetie Pie worked her way through the third grade, the fourth grade, and all the way up, until even the big, muscle-bound farm boys in eighth grade parted in the middle of the hallway when Sweetie Pie came walking through.

Some twenty years of chain smokin' and binge drinkin' later, Sweetie Pie was as hard as nails. *Webster's Dictionary* could have defined words like "mean" and "savage" just by showing a picture of Sweetie Pie. People around Cadaver would have understood what those words meant immediately. Sweetie Pie was so cruel, people were happy to hear that she had joined the Outlaws Motorcycle Gang. Maybe her new friends would have a moderating influence on her life.

It was in the Outlaws Motorcycle Gang that Sweetie Pie met Snake Schwanz, a squeaky little mouse of a man. They were meant for one another. *Sweetie Pie needed a man and, with all the scrapes the Outlaws got into, Snake needed protection.*

But not everybody considered it a match made in heaven. There was considerable resistance when Sweetie Pie brought Snake home to her parents. "Hi, Mom and Dad, this is my boyfriend Snaaaake. Ain't he cute?" Well, let me tell you, Betty May took one look at Snake with his black leather jacket, his ten-foot logging chain hanging on his shoulders, that big gold ring in his nose, and she threw Snake and his motorcycle right off the porch.

Before Sweetie Pie could even begin to defend Snake, Ralph was all over him like a cheap suit, grabbing him by the nose ring. "Ya got a job? You gotta good job? Or are ya just a stinkin' free-loader?"

Finally, Sweetie Pie wedged herself between her dad and her weasel-shaped, trembling boyfriend. "Come on, Pops, don't sweat the small stuff. Snake's been thinking about getting a job. He's got a real good chance to get a part-time job at McDonald's! One of these days he's gonna apply!"

In the end, Ralph and Betty accepted the inevitable. Sweetie Pie and Snake were getting married, and there was nothing they could do about it. They reluctantly consented, but only after reminding their daughter of the immortal words of the great Greek philosopher Socituya: "Ya make yer bed, ya gotta lie in it."

Trouble followed the young couple like stink follows a skunk. Sweetie Pie and Snake had a very unorthodox view of church etiquette. Snake didn't care much for rings, except for the ring in his nose. He wanted to exchange new motorcycles instead. Sweetie Pie was in favor of that, but Betty May put her foot down and threatened to stop payment on the wedding. When Betty May got her tongue oiled up, not even Sweetie Pie, Snake and all their friends in the Outlaws Motorcycle Gang wanted to argue. They knew they'd all be chopped liver if they took on Betty May. Shotguns, chains, num-chucks, and even pepper spray wouldn't do much against a tongue like that.

It was one issue after another when Sweetie Pie and Snake met with Willie to plan their wedding. Resigned to the fact that they had to exchange rings, Snake suggested having his two boxer dogs, Trixie and Dixie, as ring-bearers. Sweetie Pie didn't want an organist or soloist, but wanted Steppenwolf's "Born To Be Wild" played over and over again during the wedding. She explained that it was "their song."

Pastor Goodenough searched for the courage to say no to both requests, but came up empty. He knew that the motorcycle gang was waiting outside to make sure everything went the young couple's way. He went to the window, took one look at all that leather and all those chains outside and said, "Sounds all right to me, but I'd better have this okayed with the Church Council."

The next crisis came at the wedding rehearsal when Sweetie Pie led Snake into the church by his ten-foot logging chain tied to the dog collar around his neck. That's how they wanted to march down the aisle at their wedding! But Betty May put her foot down again. Why, this was the first time in twenty years her daughter Sweetie Pie would be wearing a dress! No way she would let her little daughter pull on a greasy, oily chain while wearing white gloves and a wedding dress!

When dawn broke the day of the wedding, Willie didn't want to get out of bed. He knew someone would have to pick up all the beer cans and whiskey bottles thrown on the church lawn after the wedding rehearsal. With the kind of party that took place on the church property the night before, no doubt there'd be some headstones switched in the church cemetery. Maybe the Outlaws had even dug up a few graves looking for nose rings and neck chains. Willie didn't dare object to their rowdy behavior while it was going on. If he had objected, he knew what they would have said. He'd heard it before: *"It's our wedding, pastor! Why can't we do whatever we want?"*

A half hour before the wedding a dozen Harley Hogs were pounding the streets of Cadaver. The wedding party was back. Pastor Goodenough trudged reluctantly to the church, thoroughly exhausted from picking up litter and moving several headstones. But he comforted himself with the thought that in just an hour or so this would all be over.

Finally the wedding started. The men were dressed conservatively enough in their leather and chains, but the women caused quite a stir. The bride and her court wore traditional wedding gowns, *but they also had matching tattoos etched into the middle of their bare backs, tattoos showing a snake curled on top of a pie.* There was a hush when they walked in, then a titter or two, and then the sound of retching coming from a couple of the officers of the Ladies Aid sitting in the back pew.

It wasn't strange that all the groomsmen collapsed during the ceremony, still feeling the effects of their party the night before. That happens at most weddings. But the way it happened was somewhat unusual. *It was as if someone had set up six dominoes to watch them all knock each other down.* The best man, a big hulk of a fellow called Man Mountain, fell backward first. He fell into Road Rage. Road Rage fell into Chain Saw. Chain Saw fell into Scar Face. Scar Face fell into Grizzly Pete. And, together, they all landed on Snake's little brother, Bear Scat.

At the exact moment those human dominoes fell, pandemonium broke loose. That's when Sheriff Bully Boy Peterson and his men rushed into the church shouting, "You're all under arrest!" Sheriff Peterson had chosen Sweetie Pie's wedding as the opportune time to conduct a sting operation, trap the Outlaws Motorcycle Gang, confiscate all the bikes they'd stolen through the years, and take revenge for the time Sweetie Pie had beat him up in the third grade.

Snake hid under the pulpit, but Sweetie Pie and her bridesmaids fought bravely. They were kicking, scratching, clawing, ear biting, eye gouging, hair pulling, karate chopping, and punching. There were knees to the groin, elbows to the stomach, and fists to the Adam's apple. Once again Sweetie Pie demonstrated the leg sweep, the atomic drop, the pile driver, the back-breaker, the body slam, and the chokehold. But it was no use. There were too many policemen, and no help from the men, who were still passed out on top of Bear Scat. Finally, the whole wedding party was hauled off to jail, except for Bear Scat, who was taken to the hospital as flat as a Peterbilt pancake. After the last paddy wagon was gone, Willie was left holding a marriage license set to expire by midnight.

When Missy came home late that afternoon, she said, "How did the wedding go, Honey? Was the bride beautiful? Did her father give her away?"

Willie said, "Just your typical wedding, dear, with lots of people acting up. *I wish people would learn to behave at weddings. Nobody seems to understand that a wedding is a sacred worship service."* That's all Willie said. It was too long a story to tell.

Chapter Eight:
The Church Picnic

Both churches in Cadaver were having their picnic at Mausoleum Park on the same Sunday. The first time they did that was some twenty years earlier, when an inexperienced park superintendent made the double-booking mistake. It didn't work out that first time or any time thereafter. But with the rivalry that existed between All Sports and Our Lady of Only Holy Desires, neither church was ever willing to change the date of its picnic.

One problem was that the two open-sided rain shelters were only six feet apart. When the 9:00 a.m. services began and the two clergymen were standing behind their portable lecterns, they were almost back-to-back. *The rival congregations, who didn't like one another very much, were sitting there glaring and making faces at one another.* And when Pastor Goodenough turned toward the makeshift altar, addressing God, he was actually staring into a hostile congregation of Catholics. It would have been enough to unnerve one of the apostles.

Willie struggled to get through the service. He fumbled the Apostles Creed because he relied on his memory in the midst of all those distractions. He even stumbled over the Lord's Prayer, much to the delight of the Catholics. Then a gust of wind blew his sermon off the lectern just when he started to preach. Before he could step around the lectern and say, "Could you please pick that up for me?" *a little Catholic boy sitting in the Lutheran section had already made it into a paper airplane and sailed it into the fifth row of the Catholic congregation.*

Every year the two churches had a "War of the Decibels." Both groups turned up their audio systems as high as possible in an attempt to drown out the rival system. People in Cadaver didn't have to go to a rock concert to ruin their hearing. All they had to do was attend their annual church picnic. Everyone's ears rang like a tuning fork after the services were over. If some fool would try to start up a conversation right after the services, the response would be: "Huh?" or "Say wha?" or sometimes a more polite "Could you please repeat that?" The person on the receiving end of the first "Huh?" or "Say wha?" would then respond with his own "Huh?" or "Say wha?" Back and forth it would go until one of them would finally give up, point stupidly at his ears, and walk away.

As soon as their services were over, the Lutherans ran to their beer tent and the Catholics raced to buy chances for their Lincoln Town Car raffle. The women prepared the potlucks. It was left to Pastor Goodenough and good old John Smiley to haul all the chairs, the portable lectern, the makeshift altar, and the winning audio system back to the church.

Willie returned to the picnic just in time to prevent a fight between the rival youth groups over who would use the baseball diamond. It was finally decided that both would use it. Each would field a team that would play against the other. It seemed like a logical compromise. Willie wondered why nobody thought of it before he got there. When Father Janski volunteered to be the umpire, everything was under control at the ball diamond and the Catholics were guaranteed a win.

Next Willie hurried to the playground where he was responsible for managing the smaller children's games. There was the fifty-yard dash, the sack race, the scavenger hunt, the softball toss, the ring toss, the bean bag toss, the horseshoe toss, and the water balloon toss. The little ones hooked plastic fish out of washtubs, ate donuts off a string, and chased cookies down with milk.

There was only one sour note played at the Kiddie Olympics. That was when old Mrs. Crabby Doolittle, the former pastor's wife, hobbled out into the middle of everything and demanded to know why Pastor Goodenough hadn't started the games with prayer like her husband Gottlieb used to do. Willie meekly bowed his head and dedicated the fifty-yard dash, the sack race, the scavenger hunt, the softball toss, the ring toss, the bean bag toss, the horseshoe toss, the water balloon toss, the plastic fish, the donuts, the cookies, and the milk to God. And with that, the games continued.

By the time the potluck was ready at noon, Willie was exhausted. He got everyone quieted down for the mealtime prayers and hurried to the bathroom to catch his breath. *He was secretly hoping an angel might appear in the bathroom to strengthen him.*

While in the bathroom Willie couldn't help noticing that some of the four letter words on the walls were misspelled. Willie thought about correcting the spellings, but what if someone caught him writing on the bathroom wall? He was a man of the cloth, a man of God! He couldn't be found putting graffiti on a bathroom wall! And the very last thing he wanted was to have an angel report to the powers above that he had done such a thing! So Willie looked around, and not seeing an angel, he quickly corrected all the spellings.

After lunch it was time for Willie to take a dip in Septic Creek. Not that he was looking forward to it! *Septic Creek was the kind of stream you didn't want to cross even on a bridge.* It was so dirty, there was always the danger that some malicious microorganism would mutate into a hideous bridge troll, reach up, and pull you in. Some of the locals laughingly compared Septic Creek to the Northern Lights, because it glowed in the dark and flowed in all kinds of undulating colors: red and green, and yellow and brown. To those who lived downwind of Septic Creek it wasn't a laughing matter. Whenever they caught a whiff, they'd say, "Ooou-weee! Septic Creek is backing up again!"

Soon it was time for the annual tug of war, the men of All Sports against the men of Our Lady of Only Holy Desires. With the rope stretched across Septic Creek, both sides pulled back and forth until both Father Janski and Pastor Goodenough fell in and were covered with some of the greasiest, smelliest ooze you'll find on Planet Earth. It happened every year that only Father Janski and Pastor Goodenough got pulled in. They never caught on. But that's how their churches got them to take turns in the dunk tank, which was a big money-raiser for both churches. There was nothing that young and old liked better than to trip the lever and send their shivering ministers into the icy water. And there was nothing those two grease balls wanted more than another rinse.

That's the way the whole day went. Like the Energizer bunny, Willie hurried from one job to another, doing everything he was expected to do. He coped with the usual drunks, the normal upset stomachs from the potluck, and the customary scuffles between the rednecks of the two churches. But finally people began to tire of it all. Most of the members of All Sports were gone when Willie called the last drunk a cab and slowly limped home.

Willie was heading for a hot shower when the doorbell rang. It was Father Janski and a contingent from Our Lady of Only Holy Desires delivering the keys to the new Lincoln Town Car. "There must be some mistake!" Willie said. "I never bought a raffle ticket for the Town Car."

"Well, maybe you didn't," came the reply. "But then somebody musta bought a ticket for ya. Your name *is* Willie B. Goodenough, isn't it?"

"Yes," Willie said.

"Well then, here are the keys to your new Lincoln!" And with that the sullen group from Our Lady of Only Holy Desires turned and stomped away.

"Honey!" Willie shouted. "Honey, come here quick!"

"What's the matter?" Missy asked.

"We won the Lincoln Town Car! We won the Lincoln Town Car!" Willie said it over and over again, looking at the keys in disbelief, and dancing around the room. "I don't know how we did it, Honey. I never bought a ticket. But here are the keys, and there it is in the driveway!"

To this day no one knows who bought the winning ticket for Pastor Goodenough. Missy's theory is as good as any. She believes it was a member of All Sports who felt sorry for Pastor Goodenough that day. Somebody noticed how the congregation put Willie into one impossible situation after another, and that person decided to do something nice for him. It was a very safe good deed, too—because it was anonymous. Nobody would ever find out who was nice to the minister!

Willie thought that it was an angel's doing—perhaps the very one who failed to show up to strengthen him in the bathroom. It had to be divine intervention. *Who but God could arrange to have a Lutheran minister win the Lincoln Town Car Raffle at a Catholic Church Picnic and prompt the Catholics to move the date of their picnic so it would never happen again?* Willie decided that from now on he'd be a little more alert in looking for such everyday miracles—something all of us might look for....

Chapter Nine:
Gone Fishin'

The longer Willie served at All Sports, the more problems he identified. There was Betty May's tongue, which every now and then mysteriously detached itself from all human pity and compassion and walked all over town spreading gossip and rumors. There were marital problems. The church treasurer didn't pay the bills. The church secretary couldn't type or keep a secret. People couldn't get along. Every church problem known to clergy was present at All Sports and every one of them avoided solution as skillfully as Willie's pet cats avoided their Saturday bath.

One day, when all those problems reached epidemic proportions, Willie's friend Freddie Plantemdeep said to him, "What's the matter, Willie? Did your wife leave you? Did the church burn down? You've been so depressed lately, I think you need a day off! You need to go fishin'!" Fishing was indeed the answer. Fishing took Willie's mind off his problems as thoroughly as if he were in another world.

Willie didn't go fishing often, maybe only twice a year. But it soon became obvious that the good people of All Sports didn't want Willie to go fishing at all. How could the pastor be on call 24 hours a day, 365 days a year if he went fishing? How would they get their money's worth if their pastor had a hobby?

There was one problem, of course: *how do you persuade your pastor not to fish when you yourselves are fishermen?* Nobody wanted to confront Willie directly and demand that he give up fishing. So they established a Fisherman's Support Group, dedicated to encouraging their own fishing but working to end the pastor's fishing. It was all very innocent. Everyone's motives were pure. It was all done to enhance and elevate Pastor Goodenough's ministry to make him a more perfect pastor.

One spring, shortly after the Fisherman's Support Group had been formed, millions of walleyes were spawning in the Styx River. It was wonderful. Walleyes, millions of walleyes just waiting to be caught, filled the river to overflowing. People in the Fisherman's Support Group were catching their limits left and right. They were fishing every day.

Willie wasn't even thinking of fishing. It was Holy Week. There were sermons to write, special services to prepare. But wherever Willie went, everyone asked him, "Been fishin' yet, Pastor?" "Get your line wet yet, Pastor?" Not that they were trying to encourage Willie to go fishing. They only wanted to know if he'd been fishing so they could report to the other members of the Fisherman's Support Group.

Willie made a mistake that Holy Week. On Wednesday afternoon, after sitting at his desk for what seemed like an eternity, Willie decided to straighten out his back. He hooked up his boat trailer and took it to the gas station to check the air in its tires. In ten minutes he was back at his desk working. But someone must have seen him drive out with his boat, because for the next few days every member of All Sports wanted to know, "How was fishin', Pastor? You get your limit, Pastor?" Willie almost sold his boat, but Freddie talked him out of it. "Willie, you *need* to get away once in a while! You can't work all the time! You know what your problem is, Willie? You don't go fishin' enough!"

That's how the war began. Willie and Freddie on one side, the members of the Fisherman's Support Group on the other. One day Willie and Freddie would go fishing. The next day it was reported all over town. One day Willie would get a new rod and reel for his birthday. The next day a member of the Fisherman's Support Group would borrow it and not bring it back. One day Willie and Freddie would go fishing in Willie's boat. The next day Willie's outboard motor would be missing. One day Willie found his boat trailer chained and padlocked to a tree in his back yard. Another time he launched his boat and it sank, because someone had removed the drain plug in back. *It was painfully obvious that the Fisherman's Support Group didn't want Willie to go fishing.*

Freddie suggested that Willie park his boat in plain sight and never move it. He should keep his fishing tackle in his car, leave the house in a white shirt and tie and change clothes at Freddie's house. Then they would fish in Freddie's boat, and no one would ever know. It didn't work for long. The enemy soon learned that Willie was fishing in Freddie's boat.

Freddie had one more trick up his sleeve. One day he said, "Willie, I've got it! You know that ice-out contest we have in Comatosa? They dress up those two dummies Pete and Joe in Hawaiian shirts and set them out on the ice in a boat. People bet on when the ice will break up in the spring. The ice breaks up, the boat trips a timer, and the one who guesses closest to ice-out time wins prizes. Let's dress up like Pete and Joe and float down the river. If we hook a walleye while going past a boat belonging to the Fisherman's Support Group, we'll just cut the line and stay motionless. Nobody will ever know."

It didn't work. The first time they pretended to be Pete and Joe and they floated past one of the Fisherman's Support Group's boats, they both tied into monster walleyes and neither one could bear to cut the line. They were recognized immediately. "That's it!" Willie said. "I'm never going fishing again!" And he didn't for the rest of the year.

The next spring the ice went out. Pete and Joe, dressed smartly in their Hawaiian shirts, tripped the timer. But then the rope anchoring their boat broke, too. There the two dummies went, floating down the river, dodging ice floes and looking like they were people who were fishing. Two miles down river their boat mysteriously capsized. *Pete and Joe were flung headlong into the water with hundreds of Fisherman's Support Group binoculars and video cameras trained on them.*

One of the more compassionate among the on-lookers dialed 911 on his cell phone. "Our pastor is drowning! Our pastor is drowning!" Soon there were dozens of rescue boats in the river dodging ice floes. There were divers and corpse-sniffing dogs out there dodging ice floes. There were helicopters circling above dodging ice floes. But Pete and Joe, weighted down with bricks in their britches, couldn't be found.

You can imagine the shock on Sheriff Bully Boy Peterson's face when he came to tell Missy that Willie had drowned, and Willie answered the door. Not only the sheriff, but the whole Fisherman's Support Group were somewhat disappointed that Willie and Freddie hadn't drowned. "You mean we're all out here endangering our lives and dodging ice floes for nothing? You mean there aren't any bodies in the river? What a waste of time! Why, that no-good minister of ours! If I could get my hands on him right now, I'd drown him myself!" That was the kind of anger that spread all over Cadaver because of all the trouble people thought Willie had put them through.

Quicker than you can say, "Kill the minister!" a mob began to march toward the parsonage. There were ropes to hang Willie, stones to stone him, whips to whip him, chains to flog him, buckets of water to drown him, plastic bags to smother him, hot tar and feathers to hot tar and feather him. People stood outside the parsonage shaking their fists and shouting obscenities.

Willie heard the noise and briefly glanced out the window. "Oh, isn't that sweet! Missy, you have to see this. The neighbors are all gathered here at the house praising God that I'm safe!"

He never found out that the neighbors were angry, because just then a small earthquake shook the town. Willie and Missy dove under the kitchen table until it was over, and the mob scattered. *None of the members of the Fisherman's Support Group realized that it was the Lord Himself firing a warning shot under their feet.*

Meanwhile, the Fisherman's Support Group weren't the only ones who had mistaken Pete and Joe for real human beings. The walleyes that ruled the depths dragged Pete and Joe to the bottom of Davey Jones' Locker. There the mad scientists among them conducted ingenious experiments analyzing the two "humans" who had fallen into their finny clutches. Their research was conducted with the hope that someday every fisherman might meet the same fate as Pete and Joe. But they soon realized that they were wasting their time on Pete and Joe. Pete and Joe weren't human. They needed real humans for their experiments. *"Tomorrow!" they said to one another. "Tomorrow we'll get our fins on some real humans! Pity the poor humans who go fishing tomorrow!"*

Later that night, Willie and Missy were sitting around the fireplace talking about the day's events. Missy said, "Oh, Willie, I'm so glad it wasn't you in that boat. I'm so glad you didn't drown." Then she paused for a moment and said, "You know, Willie, what happened out there today reminds me of what happens in the church. Think of all that activity: hundreds of people lining the shore, dozens of boats, divers, corpse-sniffing dogs, and helicopters circling above. And nobody was rescued, Willie! Nobody was rescued!"

"Think of all the activity in the church! Meetings in the church basement, meetings in the Mother's Room, secret meetings at the town hall and in the taverns! People arguing about the new hymnal, what color the welcome mat should be at the church, or what kind of candles we should use on the altar. No matter when you enter the church, there's activity. One group is repairing the roof. Another group is having a dart ball game. *But nobody is studying God's Word. Nobody is being saved, Willie. Nobody is being saved!* What are we going to do, Willie? What are we going to do?"

"I don't know, Honey," Willie said. "I've had it. I'm going fishing with Freddie tomorrow! There are millions of walleyes out there just waiting to be caught. Freddie and I are going to get a few."

"But if you do that, Willie, there still isn't anybody being saved."

Chapter Ten:
Living in a Parsonage

Steam was rising from Missy's normally calm and placid face. She was really upset. "What's the matter, Honey?" Willie asked.

It had to be that old retractable lamp acting up again, the one that hung over their kitchen table. It fell at the most inopportune times. It was so dangerous they called it "the guillotine lamp." It had crushed birthday cakes, mashed potatoes, sliced roast beef, chopped liver, carved turkey, diced carrots, cut cabbage, sawed coconuts, and word was that old Pastor Gottlieb Doolittle had used it to cut the heads off his chickens.

But humans were the guillotine lamp's preferred prey. More than once, when Willie was reaching for the sugar, it almost claimed his fingers. Willie learned to feint toward the sugar first. He would pretend to be oblivious to his surroundings, blithely reaching for the sugar, but then quickly pull his hand back just as the guillotine lamp fell. Once it fell, the sugar was his. But then, of course, Willie could also figure on a good half hour of physical effort and a steady stream of ominous threats before the lamp retreated to the ceiling again.

"No, it's not that cursed lamp this time," Missy said, wiping away tears. "It's everything else in this run-down, ramshackle house. I was making a casserole for supper tonight, and the circuit breaker tripped four times! When are the trustees going to check the wiring? Someday there'll be a fire, we'll be in bed sleeping, and we'll be dead!"

"Now, now, calm down, Honey. The trustees know about the wiring. Come on. Let's just sit down and eat supper. Everything will be okay."

"Boo, hoo, hoo! ... Boo, hoo, hoo, hoo, hoo!" Once again Missy burst into tears. "You don't understand, Willie! There is no supper! There is no casserole! You know how crooked the kitchen floor is and how slanted the table is because of it! When I put the casserole on the table tonight, the dish slid down the whole length of the table. It hit the floor and broke into a million pieces! That was my best casserole dish, Willie. We got it for our wedding. And now I don't have anything for supper! I hate this parsonage, Willie! Why can't we have our own home like everybody else? Boo, hoo, hoo. ... Boo, hoo, hoo, hoo, hoo."

Actually the parsonage at All Sports wasn't all that bad as far as parsonages go. It was a little two-bedroom house with plenty of room for three people. Yes, the lamp over the kitchen table was a problem. Yes, the electrical system was a fire waiting to happen. Yes, there was a noticeable fifteen-degree slope to one corner of the kitchen floor. But the parsonage also had its good points. There was a stately, gaping hole in the north overhang that provided a home for a couple of dozen bats. And there was a majestic crawl space under the porch that sheltered everything from stray cats to rabid skunks. Every spring Willie and Missy watched one family of critters after another emerge from under the house. It was wonderful! The parsonage was a little Noah's Ark, providing shelter for all kinds of living creatures!

Not a problem at all, until the year the hole under the porch housed a badger family! Mama Badger was so ornery, so protective of her little ones, that nobody could get near the front door. Mail had to be delivered a half block away. Fed-Ex and UPS refused to deliver, claiming there was no such address in town. People refused to come to the parsonage for counseling. It was just too dangerous. Even Willie and Missy had to be sure Mama Badger wasn't home before they made a dash for the back door.

If people were looking for someone to blame for the dilapidated condition of the parsonage, it wasn't hard to identify the culprit. All Sports' head trustee was a man named Mo Crastinator. Year after year, he accepted the sacred responsibility of repairing and maintaining all of the church's property, but he just never got anything fixed at the parsonage.

By all other standards, Mo was a wonderful man. He was as pleasant and easy going as anybody could be. He was conscientious, detail-oriented, and industrious to a fault. He was always working. And the problem certainly wasn't a lack of concern! When he heard about the electrical problems at the parsonage, he was so concerned he rewired his own house twice. When he heard about the slant in the parsonage kitchen floor, he bought jacks and oak timbers and made sure his own kitchen floor was level. When he heard about the guillotine lamp, he replaced his own retractable lamp. When he heard about all the critters that called the parsonage home, he nailed down every board and shingle at his house. Then he put up a chain-link fence around his property to keep critters away. Mo Crastinator was so conscientious, so concerned, so busy preventing problems at his own house, he had no time to take care of the parsonage.

Time and space would fail if we tried to list all the perplexing problems that drove the occupants of the parsonage crazy: the dirt floor in the basement that turned into quicksand when water seeped in after a rain, the leaky windows that sucked clouds of mosquitoes into the house in the summer, the cranky furnace that refused to kick in once the outside temperature reached ten below, the pint-sized hot water heater that only spit out enough hot water for one quick shower, and the old hand-me-down, one-room air conditioner that was so loud that all the dogs in the neighborhood howled when it was turned on!

In spite of its deficiencies, the people of All Sports were extremely proud of their parsonage. In their minds, it was a mansion, a castle fit for a king. In fact, *they considered the free housing they provided to be such a good deal for Willie that they subtracted $8,000 from his salary every year just to keep him from getting too far ahead of them financially*. And it worked! Lord knows, Willie wasn't gettin' ahead at all.

About the time Missy reached her wit's end concerning the parsonage the good people of All Sports were preoccupied with a different problem. The area around Cadaver hadn't received measurable rain for almost six weeks. People's lawns and gardens were burning up. Farmers were worried about their crops. People requested prayers for rain on Sunday. Many demanded that Willie pray for rain in his personal prayers. "Pastor, you've got connections we don't have. It's up to you to make it rain."

One farmer told Willie that if he didn't get a corn crop that year, he could hardly support a raise for Willie in next year's budget. "It's up to you, pastor. But you can do it. You've got connections!"

Not for one minute did Willie think he had any better connections than anyone else. But if next year's raise depended on bringing rain to

Cadaver, he knew he'd better start prayin'.

For one solid month prayer was job number one for Willie. He prayed before he got out of bed in the morning. He prayed while shaving. He prayed while brushing his teeth. He prayed in the shower. Willie prayed on every step leading into the church, in every pew, at the lectern, in the pulpit, at the altar. And being tempted to suppose the Catholics were right about praying through saints, Willie even said a hurried prayer before each one of the 152 headstones in the cemetery. He prayed so earnestly in the cemetery that his sweat was like great drops of blood falling to the ground.

But after a month of steady prayer, still no steady rain. *Not one drop of precipitation resulted from all the sweat, all the labor, and all the calluses that Willie developed on his knees.* Not one threatening cloud appeared in the sky.

There were other threats in abundance. People threatened to quit the church. They threatened to withhold their offerings. They threatened to get a new preacher if Willie couldn't make it rain.

Finally, one day Willie told Missy about all the unrealistic expectations and all the threats, how the people were ready to freeze his salary, quit the church, and even string him up if he didn't make it rain. "Don't worry, honey. God will provide. I'll pray about it," Missy said.

The next day it rained. A glorious, gully-washing rain. It rained cats and dogs in the morning, pitchforks and hammer handles in the afternoon. And the day after that it rained again. People were so proud of Willie and his connections! But after two weeks of steady rain the Styx River was flowing through the streets of Cadaver. Everyone's basement was flooded. Caskets were bobbing up out of the ground in the cemetery and floating down the river.

Again, there were threats, threats to lower Willie's salary, threats to get rid of Willie, threats to leave the church, even threats that visitors would join the church. Willie prayed night and day, but still it kept raining.

Then one day, after a third week of steady rain, Willie and Missy were standing on a hill overlooking Cadaver. As they watched, the parsonage floated down the river. They were surprised to see Mo Crastinator swimming after it with tool belt in tow, vainly trying to save it. They steadfastly watched until both Mo and the house had floated out of sight. Willie and Missy had saved their baby and all their earthly goods. But the house was gone.

But Missy didn't seem to mind! As soon as the house was out of sight, Missy pulled out a packet of papers and said, "I don't think we're going to miss that old shack, Willie. Just sign here. You've been so busy with all your church work I took a few things into my own hands the last couple of days. *Yesterday the bank approved a loan for us. We move into our own home tomorrow.* It's a wonderful, modern home built upon a hill above the flood plain with lots of room so we can have more children. I can't wait to show it to you!"

Then Missy got very quiet. She leaned against Willie, took his hand, and spoke to him very softly. She said, "But Willie, one more thing. Prayer does work, you know. It works for me! Otherwise, we'd still be living in that miserable, old, run-down parsonage. But if prayer's going to work for you, you gotta believe in it, Willie. You can't just go through the motions. You gotta believe in it. *You have to believe the Lord will give you whatever you ask for, as long as it's good for you.*"

Chapter Eleven:
The Youth Group Campout

By his seventh year in the ministry, Willie had embraced the unassailable truth on which all the great philosophers of every civilization were agreed: young people were nothing but trouble. Willie knew that you had to look past the sweet and innocent face on the outside and beware of the sneaky evils that lurked on the inside. As the great sophist Sly Nitpicker once said: when surrounded by teenagers, one needs to reposition himself promptly lest he be swallowed up in a sea of idiocy and malice.

Was this ancient, well-established assessment too critical of teenagers? Not at all! Everyone knows that young people are "tweeners." They are people suspended far too long between the cherished goal of maturity and the handy excuse of immaturity. They pretend to know how to save the world, but they cannot even fend for themselves. They're like robins, full grown, but still sitting in the nest and chirping, "Feed me! Feed me!" They are like little pigs refusing to leave the trough. If only they could be polite little robins and agreeable little pigs, but they seem compelled to quarrel with every opinion their parents dare to express! They constantly rebel and they undermine the establishment in every way they can.

When ten or twenty such tweeners gather together in the church, they are called "A Youth Group." But lest the reader panic at the thought of having all that evil together in one place, please understand that in the church these intelligent and opinionated creatures act as if they don't have a brain cell among them. In the church young people can't decide what to do or when to do it. They forget their money and lose their permission slips. If elected to an office, they cannot function. In the church young people are helpless and even feckless—most of the time, at least.

The Youth Group Campout was only hours away. Willie was about to spend two full days with some very annoying humanoids, and there was no way out! Willie took one look at the list of people signed up, and a cold sweat broke out all over his body.

Signed up for the campout were some of the worst scoundrels he had ever had in Confirmation Class. On the list were Wascally Wobert, who still had trouble saying his *R*s and D-D-Derelict D-D-Dave, who stuttered when he was caught doing something wrong. There was Malicious Marvin, Feisty Fred, Ruthless Randy and Hoodlum Hank. A fine group of reprobates.

The girls, on the other hand, were some of the sweetest young ladies that Willie had ever known: Barbara Babycakes Benelli, Susie Sweetheart Steinhofer, Pretty Polly Prichard, Holly Honeybunch Happenstance, and Lovely Linda Lightsout. Last on the list, and sure to be pushed out of the car at the last minute and forced to go on the campout against their will, were Prissy Pearson and her brother Billy the Nerd Pearson.

The night before the campout Willie couldn't sleep. He thought about the year the kids put poison ivy into the counselors' sleeping bags. Then there was the time someone brought a whole duffle bag full of rubber snakes and spiders. At the oddest moments people would suddenly stop, stare stupidly at the ground ahead of them, scream at the top of their voices, and then turn and run full-bore into trees and over cliffs. Or they would jump out of their sleeping bags, frantically brush themselves off while running in place for a few seconds, and then dash off into the darkness, screaming and howling at the moon.

One year the kids stole the counselors' mosquito spray. After twenty-four hours of non-stop slapping, scratching and itching, the counselors were so drained of blood that old Doc Sudalot was called in to administer blood transfusions. Rumors are still circulating that the blood Doc used came from a local funeral parlor, because for years the poor souls who received that tired blood complained of a lack of energy.

Every year it was a war out there. Every year one or two counselors were carried out by stretcher or flown out by helicopter to the nearest hospital.

Willie didn't know what would happen this year. But seeing who was signed up for the campout, there was one very disturbing question pacing the corridors of Willie's mind: How was he going to keep those nasty boys away from those sweet and innocent girls?

Finally, at about 2:00 a.m., Willie dozed off, only to be wakened by a pounding on the door. It was Guido Benelli and two other rough-looking men dressed in pinstriped suits. "Here, Reverend. Here's a ham for you and the Missus. Me and the boys just stopped by to remind you how important it is that nothing happens to my little Babycakes on the campout tomorrow. I've heard that some of the boys who are going along have quite a reputation. So here's a little warning for you, Reverend. *Don't* let any of those rats touch my little Babycakes, or the next time my boys stop over they won't be bringin' hams—they'll be breakin' legs! *Capiche?*"

Willie didn't sleep a wink the rest of the night. When morning came, his eyes were still stuck in stark-terror, I've-seen-my-whole-life-pass-before-me position. Missy pushed his eyeballs back into his head. She forced his eyelids down and got him looking somewhat normal. But no matter what she did, she couldn't fix his nervous tic.

In the morning, those signed up for the campout began to gather in the church parking lot. One look at the chaperones, and you could see that Willie wasn't the only one who had been visited by Guido Benelli and his men that night. The Youth Group's departure was put on hold as Missy pushed the other chaperones' eyeballs back into their heads, forced their eyelids down, but failed to stop their nervous tics. There was one other small delay. Predictably, Billy the Nerd Pearson scraped his knee when his mother pushed him out of the car. To stop his crying, Billy's mother had to return home to fetch his security blanket. But with Billy's security blanket safely on board, the Youth Group was on its way.

Two hours later, thirteen hyper young people and four already exhausted counselors climbed out of their cars, unpacked, and put up the tents. Finished with that, the tired counselors crawled away to hide and catch up on their sleep. And as soon as they were asleep, tucked away behind a rock or bush, the boys quickly applied the necessary duct tape to render them helpless. They never woke up! It was too easy.

But Willie didn't go down easy. For Willie, sleep deprivation was as normal as bugs on a windshield. That's where his seminary training came in. All the late night beer guzzling, card playing, and bull sessioning had prepared him for this. Willie wasn't tired. He was just getting his second wind.

So when the Youth Group boys—hereafter referred to as "the villains, rascals, knaves, scoundrels, rogues, blackguards, reprobates, scamps, and juvenile delinquents"—when these villains, rascals, knaves, etc. tried to overwhelm Willie, they had a fight on their hands. They surrounded Willie so he couldn't get away. But Willie quickly fashioned a makeshift cross with two sticks. Remembering how it was done in the movies, Willie thrust it into his attackers' faces, expecting them to fall backwards to the ground helpless and whimpering.

It didn't work! The villains, rascals, knaves, scoundrels, rogues, blackguards, reprobates, scamps, and juvenile delinquents—hereafter for the sake of brevity referred to as "the boys"—quickly overpowered Willie and were busy wrapping him in duct tape when two of Guido Benelli's men suddenly appeared out of nowhere with guns drawn and stopped them. Then it was the boys' turn to be fashionably draped in duct tape.

Smothered in tape and tied to trees, they were defenseless against waves of blood-sucking mosquitoes. Giant woodpeckers hammered on the trees they were tied to and vibrated the braces right off their teeth. Worst of all, they couldn't escape Pastor Goodenough's daily devotions. Between the mosquitoes, woodpeckers, and Pastor Goodenough, those six boys learned more about religion in two days than they had learned in three years of Confirmation Class.

Meanwhile, the girls and Billy had a wonderful time. They went swimming, played miniature golf, went hiking, played volleyball, conducted a scavenger hunt—in short, they had more fun than a gang of mice running loose in a cheese factory.

A week after the campout, when Willie was sleeping at about 2:00 a.m., he was suddenly awakened by a knock at the door. *It was Guido Benelli, his two bodyguards and ... Billy the Nerd Pearson!* Like the other three, Billy was dressed in a pinstriped suit and packing a gun! Willie wanted to run. But Guido stopped him. "Here's another ham for you and the Missus, Reverend. I want to thank you for all you did for my little Babycakes on the campout. She met the nicest young man. I have a feeling young Billy here is going to be an important member of the family."

"Ah ... thank you, Mr. Benelli!" Willie replied. "But Mr. Benelli, could I ask you something? How did you know your boys would have to help? How did you know we counselors would be getting the worst of it?"

"Reverend, I've got eyes and ears everywhere that tell me whatever I need to know. But to answer your question, you happen to be livin' with the eyes and ears that told me you're *always* needin' a little help."

The next day Willie got a thank you note from Billy the Nerd's mother: "Thank you, Reverend, for what you did for my son. I want you to know he's abandoned his pacifier, stopped sucking his thumb, and thrown away his security blanket. He's learning how to dress himself. And he's actually showing an interest in girls! Whatever happened on that camping trip was nothing less than a miracle. But Reverend, now we have a different problem. Could you please do something about Billy's attitude? Now he disagrees with everything my husband and I say!"

Weeks later, Willie was still complaining about all the trouble he had on the campout and how nasty the boys were and how he hated dealing with tweeners. Missy listened for a while and then finally broke her silence. "Willie, face it. Your thinking is warped! *You may not like young people very much, but God loves them an awful lot. Jesus died for them, too, you know. Jesus died for them, too.*"

Chapter Twelve:
The Building Project

When Death Bed, Inc., built a casket-making plant in Cadaver, the town finally came to life. Not only were thousands of cold bodies provided fancy boxes in which to rot comfortably, but hundreds of warm bodies were given good-paying jobs. Soon there was a new supermarket, a new gas station, and a new theater in town.

The town's two churches were growing, too. All Sports, especially, was bursting at the seams. A new and bigger church would have to be built. But it wouldn't be easy!

As a charter member of All Sports Lutheran, old Henry Standpat was a force to be reckoned with. Henry wasn't entirely against building something. But what Henry wanted to build was something entirely different from what the building committee had in mind. Henry wanted to build a moat around the church to keep visitors out. He wanted to stop new members from joining the church. There were too many changes being made, too many voices demanding that things be done at All Sports that had never been done before.

Whenever the subject of building a bigger church came up, old Henry Standpat always played his trump card. He reminded everyone about what happened in Transfer City just ten years before. When the Lutheran Church in Transfer City voted to build a new church, there was an exodus from that church, of Biblical proportions, similar to when the Israelites left Egypt. Most of the Lutherans who left joined the Catholic Church to avoid paying for the new church building. There they overwhelmed the few Catholic members and turned that church into a

Lutheran Church.

Seeing the Lutheran riff-raff that took over their church, the outnumbered Catholics transferred to the original Lutheran Church, where they greatly outnumbered the few remaining Lutherans. That became the Catholic Church in town. The result was that the Catholics ended up with a brand new church built with Lutheran money. To old Henry Standpat the lesson was clear: build a new church, and you'll lose it to the Catholics—after all, isn't that what happened in Transfer City?

Another opposing force to be reckoned with was Miss I. C. Coldshoulder, an old spinster who, like Henry Standpat, hated church visitors. But instead of merely ignoring visitors with a generally accepted friendly snub, I. C. actually took the initiative to tell them not to return. If the visiting family had a child that cried or even sneezed in church, she would hand the parents a note saying, "If you can't control your child during the service, don't ever bring him here again." One note like that from I. C. and a friendly snubbing from everybody else usually meant that the visitors would never return.

Trouble was, I. C. Coldshoulder couldn't be everywhere, and there were too many visitors. So in spite of Henry's warnings and I. C.'s heroic efforts, the church continued to grow. That very night the voters would meet to decide whether to adopt the building committee's proposal for a new church or to stand pat with what they had.

After a hectic morning at the church, Willie rushed home to check his answering machine. One message was from Missy: "Honey, I just called to remind you that you have to take our two lovely little kitties, Taz and Mania, to the vet today for their shots. Their appointment is at two o'clock. Don't forget! And be nice to my little kitties. Don't let some mean old German shepherd frighten them at the vet's office!"

When Willie heard that, he unraveled. A waterfall of sweat began to cascade down his back. His heart began palpitating to the tune of "Nearer, My God, To Thee." He began to suck air like a guppy. He had double vision in one eye, triple in the other. His legs quivered like a tuning fork. There was nothing Willie hated more than taking his cats to the vet.

Most of the time Taz and Mania were gentle, purring creatures. Willie even called them Speedbump and Roadkill, because he was always stepping on them. They followed him wherever he went. But if those two vicious tigers heard just one link of a cat leash gently tap against another link, they knew they were about to be taken to the vet.

They knew they would be dragged into that awful waiting room with all those vicious dogs and other vermin and forced to endure the cold steel of the vet's needle. Taz and Mania were more than ready to drain the blood from any poor soul who would try to drag them into that house of horrors.

In his haste, and thinking about the voters meeting that night, Willie made a terrible mistake. He dropped a cat leash. Though the sound was barely audible to him, to the cats it was like the sound of a cannon. Immediately they were gone. Gone as if they had never existed. Willie looked for them until two o'clock, but never found them. Taz and Mania had more places to hide than fleas on a black lab.

It was just as well, of course, because Willie had an important voters meeting to prepare for. That night the voters of All Sports would decide whether or not to build a new church! Willie had far more important things to do than take his cats to the vet.

When the meeting began, Henry Standpat and I. C. Coldshoulder were sitting in the front row, surrounded by a large group of supporters. The building committee and its small group of supporters were greatly outnumbered. It didn't look good for the building project.

Willie opened the meeting with prayer, but he may as well have been checking for an echo at the bottom of a well. Nobody was listening. The two opposing sides were too busy glaring at one another and trading threats and insults. There was so much animosity you would have thought this was a meeting held at the city hall the day after the assessor announced that he was raising everybody's taxes.

Even some of the more loyal supporters of the building project had disappointing things to say. Tony Tightwad, the church's only millionaire, said that while he whole-heartedly supported the new church, he probably wouldn't give anything for it, because it was doubtful they'd be able to collect enough money for it anyway. The Torpedo brothers said they might be willing to give, but only if the building committee would change the plans and build what they wanted. Even the promise of plaques glued to the altar, taking note of people's contributions, failed to arouse people's generosity.

Hour after hour people took turns telling how hard up they were financially. They had no money for the new church because of their house payments, their car payments, their medical bills, the bonds they had posted for their outlaw relatives, and their gambling debts.

There wasn't one dry eye in the place when Sal Sagev got done telling about all the money he had lost the last time he had gone to Las Vegas. Sal proposed that since they were such a small, penniless group, needing to spend all the money they had for necessities, they should try to get money for a new church from outsiders through fund-raising. They could sell candles, pizzas, candy bars, Christmas cards, and pencils. The Ladies Aid could sponsor a night of black jack, Las Vegas style. Why, there was no end to the ways outsiders could be tricked into contributing for the new church.

On and on it went. Nobody talked about the overcrowding or the fact that people were being turned away on Sunday mornings. No one talked about the little children who would be lost if there were no room for them in Sunday school.

Finally, when everybody else had said his piece, Doc Heesosmart got up and said, "Having heard all this, I make a motion that we create the edifice heretofore submitted to us, and that we do it posthaste."

"All right," the chairman droned, "you've heard the motion, and it's been seconded. All in favor rise. All against the motion remain seated." Everyone in the room immediately rose to their feet, and the motion passed unanimously. *All Sports Lutheran had just committed itself to building a new church!*

That night, as Willie and Missy were sitting around the fireplace, Willie said, "Honey, I still don't understand how there could be a unanimous vote for the building project when there was so much opposition to it. You were at the meeting. What was it that so suddenly swung everybody's opinion?"

"Well, Willie, first of all, I don't think many people understood exactly what the motion was. Doc Heesosmart uses such highfalutin language that nobody ever understands him. So the people against the building project were just waiting to see what Henry and I. C. would do. When you jammed your notebook into your briefcase in disgust anticipating a rejection of the building project, Taz and Mania yowled in pain and jumped out of your briefcase where they were hiding and scared old Henry and I. C. right out of their chairs. Their supporters rose, following their lead, and it was over just like that. As I see it, the building committee owes my precious little kitties a year's supply of tuna."

Willie thought for a moment, and said, "Leave it to a couple of cats to accomplish in seconds what the building committee and I couldn't get done with months of effort! But Missy, we still have a problem. Even though everyone voted for the project, there isn't anyone committed to the project enough to give money for it. How in the world will we ever get that new church built?"

"Don't worry, dear," Missy said. "That's the way it always is in the church. We'll get that new building built. Just you wait and see. *If my two little kitties can move the project this far along, imagine what the Lord will be able to do. If He wants that new church built, it'll be built.*"

Chapter Thirteen:
The Ladies Aid

When the Crash and Burn families used the church kitchen for their family reunions, none of the twenty-four ladies in the Lutheran Ladies Aid got very excited at first. They were more than willing to overlook the fact that someone in the Crash family had broken eleven plates. None of them batted an eye when they learned that someone in the Burn family had put a hotplate upside down and burned a countertop. None of them threw a hissy fit just because the church basement smelled like stale beer and cigarette smoke. After all, things like that happened every time the Church Council met at All Sports.

No, the thing that had the ladies swarming like angry bees was the fact that their coffee was gone. The Crash and Burn families, without permission, had used up, had *stolen*, their precious stash of coffee!

This was no ordinary coffee. This was that very special coffee that Henrietta Hobs had brought back from Brazil the first time she visited the missionaries in Rio de Janeiro. When the ladies of All Sports Ladies Aid drank that coffee, it had a mysterious way of connecting them with all those wonderful missionaries in Brazil. When they smelled that special coffee, it was as if they themselves were missionaries doing mission work all over the world. They were rescuing souls from the fiery pit simply by smelling and drinking coffee! But now it was all gone! Their special coffee was gone. What would they do without it? How could they do mission work without it?

Truth be told, it was only coffee. Why the ladies got so upset about something so small was hard to understand. When the ladies were alone, they were very sweet and gentle, each one a credit to her family. But when they got together, they would swarm and sting like angry bees. What made them this way?

The queen bee of All Sports Ladies Aid was a brash, take-no-prisoners woman named Attila Dahunsky. A vicious gossip, Attila could cut a man's throat with a whisper. And she actually did that regularly. Attila would be gossiping on one side of the room, and suddenly some unsuspecting person on the other side of the room would feel something running down his neck, reach up gingerly, touch the spot, look down at his finger and find blood. Attila's tongue had lashed out across the room like a rapier and cut his throat. For years Willie thought the cuts on his throat were due to his clumsiness with a razor, until Missy explained to him what was actually happening.

George Shrink, a member at All Sports, who also happened to be a clinical psychologist, believed that what infected ladies in their sixties was something akin to PMS. It couldn't be premenstrual syndrome, of course, considering the ladies' ages, but it was similar to PMS in that it resulted in hostility and seemed to be fueled by the natural chemistry of the body. And when it flared up in one person in a room, it would usually in a kind of group-think flare up in every woman in that room. An unlucky victim, if he happened to be in that same room, might suddenly find himself under attack from dozens of tongues lashing out from all sides. He could bleed to death in seconds.

Perhaps Shrink was right. But in the end Willie knew that it didn't matter whether this was a psychological disorder, a physical ailment, or the result of an alien invasion from outer space. It simply couldn't continue. Too many victims were reaching up, touching their necks, and discovering blood on their fingers. It was the kind of trouble you didn't want in the church, and Willie was losing a lot of blood.

Then one day, alone in his study, Willie was paging through the Book of Proverbs when the proverbial light went on. He was reading the chapter about the ideal woman. There Solomon describes how the ideal woman "gets up while it is still dark ... provides food for her family ... considers a field and buys it ... plants a vineyard ... makes linen garments and sells them ... makes coverings for her bed. ..." On and on it went. But as he read all this, Willie noticed that *the ideal woman worked alone!*

Suddenly it dawned on Willie that there was no reference in the Bible to a Ladies Aid or any kind of women's organization in which women worked together outside of the family! Without checking with Missy, who was, of course, a member of the Ladies Aid, Willie raced to the conclusion that the Ladies Aids and other women's organizations in the church were dangerously unscriptural! He would have to shut down the Ladies Aid!

Very quickly Willie sat down and began to take notes, trying to record the torrent of thoughts cascading through his brain. He wrote furiously until finally the cerebral flood trickled down to the usual steady drip-drip. When the flood stopped, Willie looked down to see what he had. The pages he had been scribbling on were blank. He had absolutely no idea how to proceed. How was he going to shut down All Sports Ladies Aid?

Finally Willie came up with an idea. Maybe, if he didn't schedule their next meeting, they would forget to meet. It didn't work. They simply met without him. The next day the church basement smelled like stale beer and cigarette smoke. Even worse, in his absence the ladies had scheduled their next meeting at the exact time the Packers played the Vikings on Monday Night Football.

Willie tried again. The Ladies Aid was a service group, wasn't it? Why not suggest an unending series of service projects for the ladies? Maybe extra work would scare them off and thin out the membership. Instead, Willie found his own life ruined. Every time he turned around, he found Missy heading up the Banner Committee for the Ladies Aid, directing the kitchen cleaning for the Ladies Aid, polishing the silver communion ware for the Ladies Aid, putting up new drapes in the church basement, making layettes and booties for the new babies in the congregation, sending get well cards to the sick, and taking cookies to the shut-ins—all for the Ladies Aid. Meanwhile, Willie was busy cooking, cleaning, and washing his own clothes.

Then one day at one of the accursed Ladies Aid meetings Willie noticed the rapt attention and fawning reverence accorded the Ladies Aid treasurer and the great satisfaction the ladies got from knowing how much money they had in their treasury. $86,000! Eighty-six thousand hard-earned, fund-raised dollars that the ladies were not even thinking of spending!

"But they ought to spend it," Willie thought. "Who would want to be holding that bag with all that money when the Lord arrived for His Second Coming? Wouldn't the Lord demand to know why that money hadn't been put to use?" Willie decided that maybe, if he could separate the ladies from their money, he could shut the group down!

This time Willie challenged the ladies to spend some of their money. He suggested that they contribute to the Synod's Scholarship Fund, adopt a missionary, buy new altar cloths, put in new countertops in the church kitchen, and even install air conditioning in the church. Before making any of those suggestions, Willie wisely prepared for their rejection. He went to the meeting wearing a steel collar around his neck, cleverly hidden by his clerical collar.

But to his great surprise, the ladies were thrilled with his suggestions. They adopted them all! Of course, they had no thought of ever spending any of their own money on any of these projects, but this was a wonderful opportunity to have more fund-raisers to separate other people from their money. Willie hated fund-raisers. Everything was backfiring on him. How in the world was he ever going to do the Lord's will and shut down the Ladies Aid?

Then one day the Ladies Aid treasurer Willamena Sutton offered to go to Brazil to look for that special coffee that the ladies needed to do mission work. Luckily, they still had the old empty can so she would know what to look for. Everyone agreed that this was a good idea. So two weeks later Willie Sutton flew to Brazil with that special coffee can filled with $86,000 of the Ladies Aid money, and she never came back.

Did she get lost in the jungle looking for that special coffee? Did she lose the money somehow and feel too ashamed to come back without it? Did she spend the money on boyfriends or stay in a luxury hotel? Was she actually doing mission work with the money? Nobody knew, because nobody ever saw Willamena Sutton or the $86,000 again.

Six months later attendance at the Ladies Aid meetings had dwindled down to two people: Willie and Missy Goodenough. All Sports Ladies Aid was effectively shut down. It was as lifeless as road kill. Nobody cared, not even her majesty Queen Bee Attila Dahunsky. The ladies didn't care, because they didn't have any of their special coffee, and they didn't have their money either. Since there was no treasurer's report, they had no reason to meet.

One night, as Willie and Missy sat together in the living room, Willie could barely contain himself. He could hardly hide his glee. All Sports Ladies Aid was finally shut down! It was dead as a corpse—six feet under and pushing up daisies, as Willie's old friend Freddy Plantemdeep would say! Finally All Sports Lutheran Church would have peace and Willie could stop wearing his steel collar.

Just as Willie was about to open the Book of Proverbs and tell Missy how he really felt about the demise of the Ladies Aid, how this was what he wanted all along, Missy said: "Oh Honey, this is such a tragedy that we've lost our Ladies Aid. Who's going to do all that work now? Who's going to serve funeral meals, make new banners for the church, clean the church kitchen, send get well cards to the sick, and take cookies to the shut-ins? Who's going to do all that work, Willie? Who's going to do all that work?"

Willie gulped a larger than ordinary gulp, as he realized that his life was ruined once again. There'd be a lot more cooking, cleaning, and washing clothes in his future.

Just then Willie's eyes landed on a familiar plaque that adorned the coffee table. It championed wisdom similar to what you might find in the Book of Proverbs. It said, *"Be careful what you wish for, pilgrim. It may come true."* From that time on, Willie was a lot more careful about things he wished for.

Chapter Fourteen:
Financial Trouble

Willie had served All Sports Lutheran for more than ten years. The honeymoon was over. The bloom was off the rose. Secret meetings were being held. Muffled threats were being made. Guns were loaded. It was time for Willie to move on. Everybody knew it, everybody but Willie.

Willie loved All Sports. And he loved Cadaver. Cadaver was a nice little town in a beautiful setting, nestled along the walleye-rich Styx River, just across from Comatosa. It was a prosperous town, too, with three major industries. Death Bed, Inc. was the largest casket maker in the Midwest. Last Word Monuments was a thriving headstone maker. And Gravediggers, Inc. made a grave digging machine that was shipped all over the world. *The way Willie figured it, as long as people kept dying, Cadaver wouldn't die.* It was a great town with great people and great industry, and Willie had no plans to leave.

But Willie wouldn't provide Christian funerals for the town's atheists. And Willie had once condemned the teachings of the Roman Catholic Church on a Reformation Sunday. And worst of all, Willie kept preaching against people's pet sins. With all those special connections preachers have with the powers in heaven, why didn't he get some of those troublesome Ten Commandments cancelled? But Willie wouldn't cooperate. With Willie B. Goodenough it was "my way or the highway." People were angry. They had lost control of their church.

Still, it didn't seem right to complain too publicly when Willie rejected atheists. After all, didn't the Bible say something about God doing the same? And nobody wanted to say too many complimentary things about sin. Didn't sudden, mysterious accidents happen to people who did that kind of thing? And finally, no one wanted their saintly grandmother to know they were rejecting the church's teachings. They could lose their inheritance.

But Grandmother never objected when they railed on the one person who defended the church's teachings! In fact, in Cadaver that was the fast track to glory! Those who spoke out against Willie quickly became folk heroes. They got a lot of free drinks. There was a good-old-boy slap on the back for anyone who resented the tyranny of Pastor Willie.

Everyone agreed that Willie B. Goodenough simply *wasn't* good enough. To some he was too friendly. To others he wasn't friendly enough. He should drink a glass of beer. He shouldn't drink beer. He should spend all his time with the youth—that's where the future of the church was. He should spend all his time with the elderly—those were the people who really supported the church.

In order to retain their positions of honor in the community and their positions of authority in the church, there was only one thing the fair-minded businessmen of All Sports Lutheran Church could do. They had to freeze Willie's salary until he finally got the idea and left town. It was the only way they could regain control of their church!

The first year of Willie's salary freeze, he whimpered a bit. "Maybe I should get more education. I could get a doctor's degree," Willie told Missy. "I might even write a couple of books, and people would respect me more. How does Dr. Willie B. Goodenough sound to you, Missy?"

"Willie," Missy replied, "you've got way too much education for this place already. Four years past college is enough. And why would you want to write a book? People here don't read anyway."

When the bills began to pile up, Willie suggested that maybe he should change careers. He could get a real job, an honest job, a job where people knew he was working. With a real job he might get more than a poke in the eye on payday.

Missy would have none of it. "Willie, you have a real job. And you're already working much too hard at it. You need to spend more time with your family. Willie, you mark my words. Everything will turn out okay. The Lord will provide."

The second year of Willie's salary freeze he got a well-deserved third week of vacation, but then he was told that it had to be taken concurrently with week number two. He got a brand new health insurance plan, but when Missy looked it over, she wasn't happy. "Willie, do you realize that this new plan has a $1,000 deductible for each office visit? And this dental plan is next to worthless. Buy five root canals and get one free? Willie, nobody ever has six root canals done in a year! $10,000 for a lost limb, but only if you're born without the other one? Buy one organ transplant and get one free? Willie, this isn't an insurance policy, this is a joke! *And did you notice that if you die, the $20,000 death benefit goes not to me, but to the church?"*

The next day the pastors in Willie's circuit met for their regular monthly meeting at a church in the neighboring town of Dead Fly. Every one of the pastors attending was complaining about the reluctance of their churches to give them raises. None of them had had a raise the previous year and two had their salary cut!

In each case they tried to analyze what had happened. One of them had made the mistake of spending a small inheritance from his uncle to get a new car. The others moaned and groaned at his obvious stupidity. They lectured him with obvious derision, "Mike, didn't you know that congregations don't want their pastors driving around in new vehicles? *People think they're paying you too much if you can afford a new car!"*

Even the Circuit Pastor chimed in to scold the blundering idiot: "That's right, Mike. Congregations don't want their pastor to enjoy more prosperity than they have. You must always present an appearance of poverty. If you buy a new pair of shoes, scuff them up a little bit before you wear them on Sunday so they look old. If you buy a different car, get a can of spray paint and spray a little rust color around the fenders. But never ever—let me repeat—*never ever* let anyone know that you have a new car!"

Around the table it went. Every pastor lamented his lack of a raise. One didn't get a raise because someone on his Budget Committee didn't get a raise from his employer. Another man didn't get a raise because he had refused to bury somebody's Shetland pony. Another one was passed over because his church bulletins had too many typos.

The two men whose salaries were cut should have anticipated it. Their children were finally old enough to be in school, and their wives had gone to work. Didn't they know people would be jealous of their sudden windfall? Didn't they know their congregations would claim a portion of their wives' income by cutting their salary? How stupid could they be! Of course, it wasn't fair. Of course, their members didn't lose any of their income if their wives went to work, but who says it was ever fair?

Again, the Circuit Pastor volunteered his sage advice*: "Gentlemen, your only recourse, if your wife starts working, is to hide that fact. The congregation can't find out. Otherwise, with the congregation taking their cut and with all the other expenses involved, your wife might as well stay home."*

"But how can we hide the fact that our wives are working?" one of them stupidly asked.

The Circuit Pastor replied, "My wife wears a disguise when she leaves the house in the morning. People think her sister lives with us, and we've never corrected them. With her disguise, people don't even recognize her when they go into the store where she works."

The Circuit Pastor paused and then continued, "Gentlemen, there is one other possibility. Your wife could work at home. There's a pastor's wife not far from here who's an artist. I won't tell you who she is, but she works at home and takes her paintings to far away places like Chicago and New York to sell them. Nobody's caught on yet. So I advise you to have your wife wear a disguise or work at home, but never ever let your congregation know that she's working!"

"But my wife is a nurse," one man said.

"My wife has a degree in engineering," another one said. "Women with skills and training have to be able to use their training."

"Nope," the Circuit Pastor said. "Both your wives might as well throw away their diplomas. If they work, they'll hurt your take-home pay as long as you're in the ministry. And if they stop working while your salary is low, even for a short while to have a baby, you'll be ruined."

That night Willie told Missy about the discussion the pastors had at their meeting. When he told her she'd never be able to use her skills and be a productive member of society as long as she was a pastor's wife, Missy didn't take it very well. She was so upset she decided to take it out on the person most responsible for the unfairness at All Sports. She reached for the phone to call the chairman of the Budget Committee. Just then the doorbell rang. It was the chairman of the Budget Committee himself. Mr. Slick Pennypincher had come to talk to Willie.

As soon as Slick and Willie retired to Willie's office, Slick began wailing and sobbing so loudly that the dishes began to rattle in the kitchen cupboards. "Pastor, I'm out of a job! The casket plant is closing its doors, and 150 men were let go this morning. I'm the only one left, because I married the boss' daughter. But soon I'll be let go, too!"

While Slick Pennypincher was still speaking, the doorbell rang again. This time it was Chuckie Cheapskate, another member of the Budget Committee. He too began wailing and sobbing: "Pastor, I'm out of a job! The headstone company is closing its doors. The railroad won't ship to us anymore. Sixty-five men were let go this morning. I'm the only one left, because I own the company, but soon I'll have to let myself go too!"

While Chuckie Cheapskate was still speaking, the doorbell rang again. This time it was Leonard Loveless, the third and last member of the Budget Committee. He too began wailing and sobbing: "Pastor, I've lost my job! Gravediggers, Inc. is going out of business. There's another company that makes better digging machines than we do. Two hundred twenty men were let go this morning. I'm the only one left, because I have to sweep up when everybody's gone, but when I get 'er swept, I'll be let go too!"

All three were now wailing and sobbing in Willie's office. The noise was so deafening with all their carrying on that the walls were vibrating. Books were falling off the shelves in Willie's study. The cats were cowering under beds. And Willie didn't know how to stop the ruckus. If only he could assure his three friends that he could help them in some way, but with his salary and no raise for the foreseeable future, it was impossible. The best he could do was promise that he'd pray about it. He read them part of the story of Job, urged them not to lose their faith, and as quickly as he could, shooed them out the door.

No sooner had Willie closed the door behind them than Missy appeared with hands on hips. "I heard it all, Willie," she said triumphantly. "You see? What goes around comes around. The good Lord doesn't exactly approve when congregations refuse to give their pastors a fair and honest wage. What they've been doing to us here at All Sports isn't right, Willie. It isn't right. But God evened the score. God handled it, Willie, and we didn't have to do a thing."

Willie replied, "I understand how you feel, Honey. It does look like God had a hand in this. But there's just one problem. I'm afraid that All Sports will really cut my salary now. They'll have to. The church won't have any money, because nobody in Cadaver is employed anymore, except the bartenders and garbage men. Now they'll have a real reason to cut my salary."

Two days later, Willie got a call from his best friend, Billy Bailemout, who had dropped out of the seminary instead of graduating with Willie. Some years back Billy had started his own company making round tuits and square widgets. He was a multimillionaire now. He had a mansion in Chicago, a condo in New York, a seaside villa in Florida, and some oceanfront property he'd never seen in Arizona.

Billy was looking for a place to expand his company and employ hundreds of workers, and he was hoping that Willie might have some leads for him. Willie, of course, had more than leads. He could tell Billy about some ready-built manufacturing plants in Cadaver and some 500 workers looking for jobs! It was a match made in heaven.

When Willie told Missy about Billy moving to town and employing hundreds of people in Cadaver, Missy said, "Willie, isn't Billy your old buddy from the seminary that you're always talking about? Isn't he the one who always gives his pastor $10,000 for Christmas?"

"Yep, that's the one," Willie said.

"Well, it looks like help is on the way. Our money problems are solved, Willie. What did I tell you? *The Lord will provide, Willie. The Lord will provide.*"

"Yeah, I know," Willie said, "but I can't help wondering when the next shoe will drop around here."

Chapter Fifteen:
Sparky Dies

One day Willie noticed that his old pal Sparky wasn't acting the way he should. His bark wasn't as loud as it had once been. His bite wasn't as powerful. He was always panting. His breath was unbearable. You didn't dare get downwind of old Sparky. It was enough to water your eyes and upchuck your Cheerios. And Sparky didn't have his usual energy. He didn't run as fast as he once did. Some days he didn't run at all.

If Sparky had been a dog, Willie would have taken him to the vet and had him put down. It would have been the humane thing to do. But Sparky was an outboard motor, the only outboard Willie had, and there were too many memories. Willie couldn't discard his old pal that easily. Besides, buying a new outboard with all the money they wanted for one was out of the question.

So one Monday morning Willie affectionately loaded up old Sparky and took him to the Mercury dealer in Comatosa. If anybody could fix old Sparky, it was the owners and chief mechanics of Dead Water Marine, Righty Tighty and his wife Lefty Lucy. If anything needed tightening, Righty Tighty had the power to clamp 'er down good and tight. If anything needed loosening, Lefty Lucy could get 'er done.

A couple of days after he dropped off old Sparky, Willie began to worry. No one had called to report that Sparky was fixed. By the fourth day Willie started pacing the floor. What was wrong with Sparky? Why couldn't they get him fixed? If Sparky were a pit bull, and he resisted getting fixed, it might have been hard to get 'er done. But what was so

75

hard about fixing an outboard motor that couldn't resist?

Finally, on Saturday the call came: "Pastor Willie, your old Sparky is ready to go. You can pick him up any time." So Willie hurried over, paid the bill, and placed old Sparky into the trunk of his car as gently as if he were handling a crate of cracked eggs.

When he got home late that Saturday afternoon, Willie began to work on his Sunday sermon in earnest. Thoughts of old Sparky dying had constipated Willie's mind all week, making it impossible to dislodge any creative thoughts. But now with Sparky home and well, Willie's mind was free to function.

The sermon was finished in the nick of time. Just as Willie typed the "Amen," he looked out of the window and saw his company arriving for the weekend. It was his look-alike twin sister May B. Goodenough, who was Pastor of All-Inclusive Community Church in Diversity, Illinois. Having his sister there was bad enough, but May B. had also brought along her three dogs: Arff, Rruff, and Woof. They were the most undisciplined and rambunctious dogs that ever marked a neighbor's bushes or fouled his grass with brown deposits. And they were constantly barking. They barked at anything that moved and anything that made a sound.

That night, when everyone went to bed, Willie couldn't sleep. The dogs kept barking. They barked when a car went by. They barked when a train went through town. They barked when the moon came up. They barked when the stars twinkled. They barked when a fish jumped in the river. They barked when a bat gulped down a mosquito. The barking went on and on and on. When one dog stopped, the other two started. It was impossible to get any sleep.

Willie decided he might as well get up and do something constructive. Sure, it was Sunday morning, but he had to try Sparky out sometime to see if he was really fixed. Why not now? Why not escape to the lake? Maybe the fish were biting. He wouldn't have to listen to all that barking out on the lake.

Willie arrived at Lake Rigor Mortis at about 3:00 a.m. He launched his boat, and started old Sparky with only one pull. Yep! Old Sparky was back, with a vengeance! What power! What snap that little motor had! How sweetly he purred! How could Willie even think about getting a new motor?

"Boy, this is a new one," Willie thought to himself. "Fishing on Sunday morning! Some of the guys probably don't even have their sermons done yet, and here I am enjoying the good life out on the lake!"

Willie went straight to his favorite fishing hole about a mile from the launch and immediately started catching fish. In a couple of hours he had his limit of walleyes and a number of good-sized pan fish. Maybe he should go fishing every Sunday morning just before church. Apparently, that's when the fish bit.

Willie looked at his watch. Soon it would be 5:30 a.m. Maybe he should go back home. He had fish to clean now. And a sermon to memorize. There were special prayers to write. It was nice being out on the lake, but Willie couldn't stay any longer. Back to the salt mines. Back to his sisty ugler and her three barking dogs.

But this time old Sparky wouldn't start! Willie pulled on the starting rope again and again. But there was no response. This time there wasn't even an encouraging smoky belch, or a promising sickly cough, or a healthy cancerous cloud. There was no spark at all, not a bit of life in cantankerous old Sparky.

Willie panicked. He was a mile from the launch. He had forgotten his trolling motor battery, and his boat didn't have oars. How was he going to get home? Even if he hollered for help, who would hear him at 5:30 in the morning? There were no other boats on the lake. And besides, Willie wasn't sure he wanted to be rescued. He didn't want anyone to know that he had gone fishing on Sunday morning instead of working on his sermon.

His old fishing buddy Freddie Plantemdeep couldn't rescue him. He was out of town. Willie couldn't call any of the retired ministers in the area to cover for him. He had already used up all his vacation days. Willie's only hope was his sisty ugler. She couldn't come and get him, because she had no boat. But May B. could, maybe, take his services that morning. Other than being a little shorter than he was, she looked just like Willie. If Missy cut May B's hair so it was short like Willie's, nobody would ever know that it wasn't Willie. She could wear one of Willie's two signature ties, lower her voice a bit, and everyone would think she was Willie.

But when Willie called his sisty ugler on his cell phone to explain his predicament, she wasn't very sympathetic. She milked the situation for all it was worth. She was on vacation. She wasn't prepared. Willie and their parents never wanted her to become a pastor in the first place. What made it all right to function as a pastor now? But finally, after what seemed like hours of bickering, May B. said, "Okay, Willie, I'll take your services this morning, but it's going to cost you!"

"Anything, May B. Just name your price. I'll do whatever you ask. I just can't let the congregation find out I went fishing this morning."

It was the wrong thing to say. May B. knew she had hit the jackpot. "Okay, Willie, here's what I want. I'm getting married this fall to the love of my life, Eeza Wifebeater, and I want you to perform the ceremony."

"I can't do that, May B.," Willie said. "You know I don't like that man. He has a police record a mile long. If I perform that ceremony, it'll look like I do approve of him."

"Take it or leave it, Willie, you self-righteous loser. Who are you to tell me that my boyfriend is a bad person when you're the minister who goes fishing on Sunday morning and can't get back in time for services?"

Willie wasn't exactly negotiating from a position of strength. So he finally agreed to May B.'s terms. After that, everything fell into place. A couple of hours later a fisherman who was a complete stranger towed Willie back to the launch and never asked who he was. May B. took his services that morning, and no one in the congregation realized that it wasn't Willie up there. The only thing different that week was that wherever Willie went, people commented on what a wonderful sermon he had that Sunday, so much better than his usual.

Then the hammer fell. When May B. got back to Illinois, she sent an announcement to the whole family that she was getting married that fall to her beloved Eeza Wifebeater and that her wonderful brother Willie had consented to do the ceremony. Willie's parents, Immer B. Goodenough and his wife Shirley B. Goodenough were shocked!

They asked Willie if it was true. Was he really going to perform that ceremony? How in the name of all that's good and right could he have a part in such a thing? Willie tried to defend himself, but nothing he said made sense.

Then, as quickly as the storm clouds gathered, they began to dissipate. Willie got a phone call from his cousin Nearly Goodenough, pastor of Almost Lutheran Church in Possibility, Oklahoma. Nearly had heard about all the pressure May B. had put on Willie to marry her and Eeza Wifebeater. Nearly wanted Willie to know that some twenty years earlier, when he and May B. were in the seminary together, the two of them along with some classmates went to Las Vegas for spring break. During a wild night of carousing, May B. had married someone at a wedding chapel, and she had never gotten a divorce! Since May B. was already married, she couldn't possibly marry Eeza Wifebeater!

That was the ace Willie needed in this little poker game. This would put his conservative parents Immer and Shirley Goodenough over the edge. If May B. didn't back down, she would be disinherited. It was time to turn up the heat, time for blackmail, time to do what his sisty ugler had done to him. So he dialed her number and, like the good brother he was, presented the terms for her surrender. He promised to remain quiet about the fact that May B. was already married if the wedding were called off and May B. would never again ask him to marry her and Eeza Wifebeater. Oh, and there was one more thing. As a small token of gratitude for his silence it would be nice if Willie had a new twenty-five horse outboard motor so he would never again be stranded out on the lake.

And that, friends, is why Willie's sisty ugler backed down, how Willie got his new outboard, and how old Sparky retired to become Willie and Missy's new mailbox. But Willie learned a lesson too. *He never again went fishing on Sunday morning or at any other time when he was supposed to be preparing for ministry.*

Chapter Sixteen:
The District President

Nobody was surprised when Harry Absalom was elected District President. Any dimwit could see it coming. For years Harry was first to arrive at pastors conferences. While most of his brothers in the ministry were still rubbing sleep from their eyes, Harry was already at the conference, welcoming the host pastor to his own church. He welcomed the ladies when they arrived. He gave them big bear hugs and told them how lovely their silver hair was.

Why was Harry so early? To schmooze the little people! His firm handshakes and tender baby-kisses were the talk of the country. Nobody did it better. *In fact, politicians often watched videos of Harry Absalom's schmoozing to help them perfect their art.* But sometimes, when someone with a sensitive stomach viewed Harry's schmoozing videos, he would gag in disgust, like a cat heaving a hairball, and he would leave politics forever.

Another thing that led to Harry Absalom's election to the presidency was his energetic championing of every cause, no matter how pointless or absurd it might be. Harry assured every complainer that his grievance was just and right. People on both sides of an argument could count on Harry Absalom to support them. Harry Absalom deserved to be District President. He had made the effort. He had schmoozed everybody.

But as soon as Harry became District President, this friend of all became the friend of few. The day he was installed as President he arranged for spies in every church in the district, spies who could report anything that might reflect unfavorably on their pastor. Every sniveling snitch was handsomely rewarded with cold, hard cash. Harry had plenty of cash! For every dollar Harry paid out to a snitcher, $10 came back from a snitchee. Quicker than you can spell simony, two-thirds of the pastors under Harry's supervision were paying him monthly installments to stay in the ministry.

Besides being President of the Lukewarm District of Wisconsin, Harry Absalom was also the very popular Senior Pastor of No Principles Lutheran Church in Everything Goes, Wisconsin. *No Principles Lutheran was the fastest growing Lutheran church in Wisconsin simply because there were no principles.* While President Absalom insisted on strict conformity in doctrine and practice from all the other pastors and churches in his district, those same rules did not apply to his church. People traveled many miles to attend No Principles Lutheran to get away from all the canon law and religious regulations that were strictly enforced everywhere else. That was the secret to the tremendous growth of his church.

At No Principles Lutheran show-and-tell replaced Bible stories in the Sunday school. Everything from a butterfly to a pet pig was blessed at the altar. Burly Green Bay Packer linemen gave the sermon. Cold beer and hot pretzels were served instead of wine and wafers at Communion. "Sie Leben Hoch," an old German drinking song, was sung as a closing hymn. Priests from the local Catholic Church came in to demonstrate the latest innovations in polka masses.

Easter Sundays were really special. There was an Easter egg hunt at dawn. The children got candy. The adults found coupons for the local gambling casino in their plastic eggs. In the worship service members of No Principles Lutheran would sing alternate verses of "I Know That My Redeemer Lives" accompanied by the harp and the stump fiddle. First the harp, then the stump fiddle, and then the harp and stump fiddle together. The last verse was the best. That one was performed as a solo by Pastor Absalom himself on the spoons. It brought tears to everyone's eyes.

It was exactly three o'clock one morning when Willie's telephone rang. "Oh, oh," Willie thought to himself, as he staggered to the phone. "I hope it's not Harry Absalom. This is when he likes to call! I hope somebody died. I hope the country's at war. I hope UFOs have landed in Washington. I hope an asteroid is about to hit the Earth. I hope California is having the Big One. I hope it's Judgment Day!" Willie looked at his caller ID. Unfortunately, it was Harry Absalom on the other end.

"Hello! All Sports Lutheran Church! Willie B. Goodenough speaking!"

"Willie, this is Harry Absalom. How are you this morning?" President Absalom's gruff voice signaled that he really meant business.

"Ah ... okay, sir. A little tired, maybe. What can I do for you, sir?"

"Well, Willie, I've been looking at your file. We need to talk. I've been accumulating some alarming information about you."

"What kind of information, sir?"

"Willie, I don't know where to start. You know that Pastors Conference you missed? You never sent a doctor's excuse. And the $30 you sent me last month! You sent a check, Willie. I want cold, hard, untraceable cash. Ah, but all of that I can overlook. It's the complaints from your members that are most disturbing."

"What complaints, sir?"

"Willie, you finally got your Ladies Aid going again, right? Those ladies work their fingers to the bone trying to earn money with bazaars, silent auctions, brat sales, bake sales, and quilting parties. But a little bird told me that you're giving away some of the Bibles they purchased with their sweat and toil. You're giving those Bibles to outsiders, to people in your new member classes. The ladies aren't happy about that. *Another thing, Willie. I understand that you've been harassing families with children to get them into Sunday school. If the child would rather watch Sesame Street than hear about Jesus, what difference does it make?* Willie, you have to remember the power of Holy Baptism!"

"But President Absalom," Willie replied with a quivering voice. "Didn't Jesus say we should baptize *and teach*?"

"Not in my district, Willie. And what about that nice fellow Joe Noshow whom I transferred from No Principles Lutheran to your church? You refused to take him in. Why, Willie? Aren't my members good enough for your church?"

"But President Absalom, I never saw the guy. He never came to church. You never gave me an address where I could look for him. For all I knew, he might have been living on the west coast. All I had was a name on a piece of paper!"

"There's another thing, Willie. Two weeks ago, you were making evangelism calls in an area of Cadaver where I have members. I don't care if they do live 150 miles from my church. You're sheep-stealing,

Willie!"

"Oh, I'm sorry, President Absalom. I didn't mean to steal your members. What can I do to show you that I'm sorry?"

It was the wrong thing to say. Like a deadly boa constrictor eager to squeeze his helpless victim, Harry Absalom quickly slithered through the open door. "I tell you what, Willie. Start sending $50 a month instead of $30, and I'll forget about all of this."

"Oh, thank you, President Absalom. Oh, thank you." Willie gave a sigh of relief.

Hearing Willie's complete capitulation, Harry Absalom hung up the phone.

The next morning Willie told Missy everything. He explained that the $30 sent to the Clergy Association every month really was a bribe paid to the District President to stay in the ministry, and now he'd have to pay $50. Missy was furious.

"Willie, we're not going to do this. If you had done something wrong, I could understand it, but even then the proper thing would be to resign your ministry and not bribe the District President to stay in. And that little bird, that mole, that accursed spy at All Sports who reports all this stuff to President Absalom! It has to be Betty May Sparks! She's still upset that her husband Ralph didn't get the janitor job, and she still blames you for that fiasco at her daughter's wedding. We're not going to do it, Willie. We're not going to do it."

Two weeks later, the time came for Missy to send $50 to Harry Absalom's Clergy Association. Willie reminded her to do it, but she politely refused. "We're not going to do it, Willie. We're not going to do it."

When Willie's payment didn't arrive on time, President Absalom called. This time it was 2:30 in the morning.

"Willie, I'm missing that $50 payment. When is it coming?"

Willie was half asleep and didn't know what to say. Finally he blurted out: "Soon, President Absalom. Very soon. We're just a little short this month. We'll send it as soon as we can."

"Okay, but it better be quick if you want your name listed among the clergy a year from now."

Weeks later, Missy still hadn't sent the $50. Once again, Harry Absalom called. He was fuming. Willie had to hold the phone at arm's length so his ear drum wouldn't be broken. "Willie, you no-good so-and-so! Your ordination certificate isn't worth the paper it's printed on.

You're going down, Willie! You're going down! Last night I called the chairman of your congregation to find out when your voters meet. I'll be there, Willie. Start packing."

The day of the voters meeting arrived. It was held in the Parish Hall, a building separated from the church. As the people filed out toward the Parish Hall, you could feel their excitement. Betty May had told them that District President Harry Absalom was going to be there. People had brought their cameras, hoping to have someone take a picture of them with the District President.

And there he was. Harry Absalom himself, standing in front of the Parish Hall in a brand new pin-striped banker's suit. Greeting everybody. Hugging everybody, especially all the women. Kissing all the babies.

Willie couldn't help but notice that Harry's clinch with Missy was extra-long. After hugging Missy, Harry held both her hands very gently while the two of them looked deeply into one another's eyes and discussed whatever they discussed. Harry was probably complimenting Missy on her wavy hair and dimples. It was disgusting. Harry couldn't even leave a man's wife alone!

As soon as the meeting began, President Absalom asked Pastor Goodenough to leave so he and the congregation could discuss a very important matter privately. Willie protested vehemently, but the voters were so overwhelmed by the District President's presence and so awed by his charisma, that they quickly voted to have Willie removed from the meeting.

For the next hour Willie paced back and forth in the church. He was angry. He was scared. He was angry again. Then he was scared again. In his anger he killed every living creature he could find in the church: every bed bug, every cockroach, every mosquito, every gnat, every fly, every spider, every ant, every Asian beetle, every box elder bug, every centipede, and every millipede. In his fear Willie knelt at the altar and promised God every bit of life and every cell of his body. He would serve God faithfully every moment of every day until they poured dirt over his grave, if only he could stay in the ministry. The sixty minutes Willie spent pacing in the church seemed like eternity.

Finally, one of the elders came and told Willie he could go back to the meeting. An hour before, Willie didn't want to leave the meeting. Now he didn't want to go back. But he had to. So, like a penguin with sore feet, he slowly plodded over to the Parish Hall. *With great dread, he gingerly opened the door and stepped in, fully expecting a hammer of doom to come down on his head. Instead, he was met with loud cheers from the voters and a huge hug and handshake from Harry Absalom.* Then there was a surprise announcement from the chairman of the congregation that Willie had received a vote of confidence and had been awarded a $100 raise. Harry Absalom, who had threatened to get him fired, had convinced the voters that they weren't paying him enough! It was unbelievable! Immediately after the announcement, President Absalom said goodbye to everyone and danced out of the door. The Schmoozer was gone.

The rest of the voters meeting was a blur. Everyone was in a wonderful mood. People kept buzzing about their visit from the District President.

Later that day, when Willie and Missy reached the privacy of their home, Missy got out a bottle of champagne to toast their victory. But Willie said, "I don't understand it, Honey. Harry Absalom came here today to get me fired. What happened? Not only am I not fired, but I got a vote of confidence and a $100 raise, and it wasn't even a budget meeting! What happened in there, Missy? What in the world happened?"

Missy replied: "Willie, do you remember when Harry Absalom was hugging me and holding my hands?"

"Yes!"

"Well, I wasn't whispering sweet nothings to him. I was telling him what a dirty rat he was. You see, Willie, I did a little investigating. *I discovered that three previous district presidents had died from apparent heart attacks driving home from Pastors Conferences.* I also learned that Harry the Schmoozer had always insisted on serving coffee to the district presidents. When he helped the ladies serve their meals, he always helped with the district officers' table. I just put two-and-two together. There was too much coincidence, Willie. There was too much coincidence."

"So I told Harry that he was a dirty rat, that I was on to him, and that I was thinking about reporting my suspicions to the authorities. I told him I had no doubt that there would be three graves dug up and three autopsies conducted if he didn't behave himself at the meeting. Looks like he did behave, huh?"

"Oh, and by the way, Willie, President Absalom has agreed to send us $120 every month until four times the amount you paid him is repaid to you. *You know, Willie, the devil seems to win a lot of times, but he doesn't win 'em all!* Now, Willie, my love, let's have a little champagne before I open up a can of chicken noodle soup."

Chapter Seventeen:
Holy Dirt

It was a pile of black dirt left over when All Sports Lutheran constructed a children's playground. It couldn't stay where it was. It would have caused problems! Grass and weeds would have grown on top of it. Little feet would have climbed the pile and brought mud into the building on rainy days.

So Willie advertised free black dirt in the Sunday bulletin. And presto! After a few days it began to disappear. People filled pails, then carts, utility trailers and pick-up trucks. And before you could say, "Where did all that black dirt go?"—it was gone!

It was strange how fast it disappeared. *Stranger still were the reports that came in that there was something special about that black dirt.* Whatever people planted in it grew twenty-five times faster than things planted in other black dirt. It was the second coming of Jack and the Beanstalk. Put seed in that black dirt before you went to bed at night, and by morning it had sprouted and was reaching for the sky. Even old Stanley Greenthumb said he had never seen anything like it. People noted the special properties of that dirt and began to call it "holy dirt," because it came from the church and it obviously had miraculous powers.

Some people were quite upset when the dirt was gone, especially those who got there too late to get some. So people began to improvise. They tiptoed over to the church under cover of darkness to fill a coffee cup or to slip a little holy dirt under their fingernails from the lawn that was left. One morning, when old Stanley Greenthumb was mowing the church lawn, he drove the lawn tractor into a four-foot hole that hadn't been there the day before. He didn't see the hole, because someone had stretched a green tarp over it and sprinkled grass on the tarp.

Finally, a 24-hour guard was posted on All Sports' property to preserve the church lawn. When the guards themselves began to steal dirt, a 12-foot chain link fence topped with razor wire was erected. The church officers argued for hours whether to put the fence in front of the "Welcome" sign or behind it, but finally decided to put it in front. Even then, people kept reaching through the fence with spoons, ice cream scoops, golf ball retrievers, and chop sticks.

Meanwhile, at the Farmer's Market half a dozen stands sprang up claiming to sell All Sports Lutheran's holy dirt. Three ounces for $10 at one stand, $50 per pound at another stand.

When the good Catholics from Our Lady of Only Holy Desires got wind of the Lutherans' holy dirt, they made plans to sell some of their own. If *their* holy dirt took off like the Lutherans' holy dirt, they could forget about pancake breakfasts, tractor pulls, steer roasts, bingo, polka masses, and monthly raffles. *In their first week the Catholics sold more than $10,000 dollars of their version of holy dirt.* The Lutherans were doing everything they could to keep their dirt, while the Catholics were doing everything they could to sell theirs.

But then discouraging reports came in. Apparently, there wasn't anything special about the Catholic holy dirt. No miraculous powers. No extraordinary fertility. In fact, most plants placed in their holy dirt died, even after they were sprinkled with holy water and blessed by the archbishop.

What gave the Lutheran holy dirt such miraculous power? What gave it such fertility? Was it the leftover communion wine, reverently returned to the Lord when Mildred Greenthumb poured it on the grass just outside the church? Was it Willie's sermons? Was it his carefully chosen words, leaking out of the windows and falling gently to the earth like bird dirt? Or did a passenger plane passing in the night, going 500 mph at 30,000 feet, accidentally dump the contents of its holding tank on the church lawn? If that were the case, wouldn't some of that stuff have splashed onto the church siding? And then there was the question that had everyone scratching his head: *why hadn't All Sports' holy dirt demonstrated its miraculous powers before it was moved off the premises?* Why didn't the church lawn grow at a torrid clip, or the flowers, or the trees? Why did this amazing fertility only appear away from All Sports?

While holy dirt sales flourished, All Sports itself was dying. Willie was having trouble getting Sunday school teachers and vacation Bible school teachers. Nobody wanted to serve on boards and committees anymore. If something in the church building needed fixing, nobody had time to fix it. People were too busy selling holy dirt or planting things in holy dirt or sitting in the local watering hole swapping the latest stories about holy dirt. There wasn't any work being done at the church, unless it was done by the Goodenoughs or the Greenthumbs.

When the good people of Our Lady of Only Holy Desires found their sales dwindling, they decided they had to do something to burst the Lutherans' bubble. They took a sample of the Lutherans' holy dirt to Dr. I. Shirley Knowalot, Professor of Agronomy at Soils-Are-Us University at Tillsberg, Wisconsin, just across from Furrowsville. Dr. Knowalot analyzed the sample and found that the Lutherans' holy dirt was merely saturated with "Wondrous Grow," a common liquid fertilizer. When news of those findings came out, the run on All Sports Lutheran's holy dirt stopped. People ran to the hardware store to get bottles of "Wondrous Grow" instead.

But by that time the damage to All Sports' lawn was done. The once beautiful yard had been replaced by a gaping hole. The sturdy fence erected to protect it had been toppled. Even the "Welcome" sign had been thrown aside to steal the dirt beneath it. All Sports' yard resembled the surface of the moon.

Then one day Mildred Greenthumb came to Willie and told him that she thought her husband knew something about all this. "Call Stanley in," she said. "Talk to Stanley. He knows something. I know he does."

The next day Willie called Stanley in for a friendly chat. Within two minutes, Stanleyfound himself handcuffed to a heavy table in the furnace room, under a heat lamp, and surrounded by the church Elders. He was hooked up to not one, but two lie detectors, just in case one of them malfunctioned and proclaimed him innocent of wrongdoing.

But all that pressure was unnecessary. Stanley sang like a canary. Yep. He did it. He didn't mean to destroy the church yard. He only meant to help the church. *He saw how the members didn't seem to care about All Sports anymore. Nobody had any time for the church. If only he could get people to think about their church again, lend a hand, love their church again.* That's why he came up with this hair-brained scheme to salt that pile of black dirt saturated with "Wondrous Grow." But it all backfired. People paid attention to their church again, but in the end they destroyed it. And the Lutherans had now been completely discredited by the Catholics and by Dr. I. Shirley Knowalot from Soils-Are-Us University.

Stanley was beside himself with guilt. He begged for forgiveness. "Please forgive me," he said. "Please!" By a vote of 3–1 absolution was denied. Willie's pastoral heart compelled him to forgive, but the Elders would not be swayed. "Normally we would forgive," they said, "but not in this case."

After much thought, Pastor Goodenough, in defiance of the Elders, refused to excommunicate Stanley Greenthumb. Instead, he accepted this incorrigible, this filthy, rotten, unforgivable, penitent sinner back to the communion rail. *After all, if Stanley Greenthumb were excommunicated, who would mow the church lawn?*

When the story reached the local news, many members of All Sports began to leave the church. They were offended. In their minds Stanley had committed an unforgivable sin. He had done something they had never done. They didn't know which of the Ten Commandments Stanley had violated, but that didn't matter. In their minds, they operated on a higher plane of ethics than God did anyway.

And so they left. All the ethically superior members left All Sports. They needed to find a church that catered to people like *them*, people who had no sins to confess, people who were more spiritually self-sufficient than common rabble like Stanley Greenthumb, people less ethically challenged than Willie B. Goodenough.

Mr. and Mrs. Joe Pharisee left first. They joined the Feelgood Church. There they heard that they were as good as they thought they were. Stilla Delinquent and her family joined Lord of the Strays Community Church, because church attendance there was optional. Then Mr. and Mrs. Avaricious left, won the lottery, and never did join a church lest they be asked to share their new wealth with the Lord. It was quite an exodus. Everyone with a chip on his shoulder or a holier-than-thou attitude used the holy dirt scandal as a reason to leave All Sports with their noses in the air. How could the pastor possibly forgive Stanley Greenthumb for what he did?

But they were all happy! According to what they told their friends and neighbors, everyone who left All Sports was gloriously happy. Some of those who left even turned their lives around. Responding to the work righteousness taught in their new churches, they finally tried to be righteous.

Joe Pharisee became chairman of the Feelgood Church. At last a group of people recognized him as the leader that he always thought he was! Stilla Delinquent headed up the Sunday school at Lord of the Strays. It wasn't that hard a job, because none of the children of the church actually attended. Other no-accounts and black sheep who left All Sports chaired evangelism committees in their new churches. Some even took a handy $39.99 twenty-minute online course, certifying them for the ministry, complete with ordination papers.

Willie was dismayed. Every time he heard about people's newfound spiritual life after they left All Sports he felt like a failure. He wondered what he had done wrong.

Then, one day, Stanley and Mildred Greenthumb decided to move away. "It's not you, pastor," Mildred said. "You've been great. It's just that people here can't seem to get past what Stanley did. They just can't forgive."

So Stanley and Mildred Greenthumb moved to New Hope, Wisconsin. There they joined the Lord Our Righteousness Lutheran Church. Their faith flourished there, just as it had as All Sports. Stanley started a business in New Hope and became a millionaire. He manufactured Greenthumb Top Soil, a potting mix laced with Wondrous Grow. That's when people began to say that if you were good at growing things, you had a green thumb.

Meanwhile, Willie and Missy were still at All Sports. Missy took care of the Communion ware now, a job Mildred Greenthumb once did. Willie mowed the church lawn, along with all his other duties. *He still preached God's full and free forgiveness through Jesus, and the people of All Sports still did their best not to listen to what he said.*

Then one day Missy said: "Willie, we need to get away from All Sports. We need a new start. I think the only way we'll ever blossom is if we get away from All Sports. Just like all the people who left. They all prospered, but only after they left. Just like that holy dirt people used to sell, remember? It could only accomplish great things when it was away from All Sports. It's the same with us, Willie. *We need to get away from here, Willie. We need to get away from here.*"

One day a call came. It was an opportunity for Willie to be a hospital and prison chaplain. Willie could stay where he was, serving at All Sports, or he could accept the new position as a chaplain. Thinking it over, Willie decided there wasn't much difference in the two responsibilities. In both cases, he would be taking care of people who were sick and criminally insane.

But Missy pointed out that Willie would double his salary if they moved. He'd make $60,000 a year as a chaplain, compared to only $30,000 at All Sports. Missy said, "Willie, here's our chance to get braces on the kids' teeth. You can get new glasses—and Lord knows you could use a new suit!"

But Willie was adamant. "Missy, if I take this call and make twice as much—and the people of All Sports find out – they'll think I wasn't dedicated. They'll think I'm in the ministry for the money."

So Willie declined the call to be chaplain and stayed at All Sports. And what was the reaction of the people of All Sports when they found out? In the immortal words of the All Sports elders: "Normally we would forgive, but not in this case." *Good thing Missy was there to remind Willie every day that even if people don't forgive, God does.*

Chapter Eighteen:
Missy's Friends

Missy Goodenough was a busy gal. Besides caring for two active children, she answered the phone for her husband, typed the Sunday bulletin, taught Sunday school, critiqued Willie's sermons with or without his request, and made cakes and hot dishes for the many fellowship hours and potluck meals at All Sports.

But for all her activity, there were times when Missy was as lonely as a weathervane heifer sitting on top of a barn. When she sat down at a table in the Fellowship Hall, no one sat next to her. No one talked to her, unless they were trying to dig up a little dirt on the Goodenough family.

Why didn't people like her? Why wouldn't they sit next to her? Did she have B.O. or bad breath? Missy tried deodorants and cheap perfumes. She gargled with every mouth wash that was sold. But it was no use. She couldn't get Willie to stay away, but everyone else did. She could be in a room full of people, but she was still all alone.

Then, suddenly, three women showed an interest in Missy and changed everything. They were wonderful. They were tremendously encouraging, especially when Missy and Willie were having a spat and Missy needed someone to talk to. If the Goodenoughs got a letter of inquiry from the IRS, if Willie's black sheep Uncle Never Goodenough was stabbed in a bar fight halfway across the country, if their son Kenny B. Goodenough got into trouble at school pulling someone's pigtails, Missy knew that she had three friends she could safely confide in: Tracy Traitor, Vicky Vicious, and Lucy Lipps. They were the most wonderful friends she could ever have hoped for. They listened. They sympathized. They spent time with her. Together, the four friends went shopping, had afternoon tea parties, and took turns babysitting each other's children. They were inseparable.

Good thing Missy had those special friends at All Sports, because Willie's life had taken a turn down Calamity Street. A number of shut-ins had died, one after another, and word was that Willie had put poison in the communion wine. Offerings were down, and word was that Willie was sneaking into the church safe at night and skimming money off the top before the offerings were counted. All kinds of charges were being made. Willie was the main topic of every conversation, and, like always, completely unaware of it.

But in this time of unparalleled trouble, Missy's friends came to the rescue. Entirely on their own, they began an investigation of the charges against Willie. Some would call it gathering evidence. Getting to the bottom of things, others would say. But Missy's friends were far more direct. They just wanted to bring fire and brimstone down on the guilty.

Tracy Traitor and her husband Perpa Traitor had never met a minister they liked. Ministers were always shoving religion down peoples' throats, making people think about God and where they were going after they died. There was no excuse for that kind of behavior. It was especially inappropriate for Willie to question anyone's morality with all the things he was doing.

It took courage and a lot of ethical planning to quietly sneak into the pastor's house unnoticed like Tracy did. But one day, sort of by accident, as she explained it, she found herself alone in the pastor's house. She used that God-given opportunity to take some communion wine from Willie's private communion set.

The results of her investigation were stunning. When Tracy gave Willie's communion wine to her baby kittens, they collapsed in a heap. When she gave some to her pet parakeet, it died. *Pastor Goodenough had indeed put poison in the communion wine!* As soon as Tracy realized she had the goods on Willie, she told everyone.

Vicky Vicious worked at the local bank. She was able to monitor the Goodenough's bank deposits. She purposely overlooked the extra checks Willie received, the mileage payments All Sports made to Willie and the gratuities from weddings and funerals. With those omissions she could gleefully report that every month Willie Goodenough was depositing more money than his salary could account for. *So it had to be true.*

Willie was indeed sneaking into the church safe at night skimming money off the top before the offering was counted. Vicky too began to tell everyone what she knew.

Lucy Lipps didn't care about the shut-ins dying or the money missing. She wouldn't have cared if Willie had been some kind of serial ax murderer. What blew her cork was the fact that All Sports reimbursed Willie for business mileage. She resented every penny that was paid. Her husband was a farmer. He didn't get reimbursed for all the miles he made, walking from the house to the barn, from the barn to the house, trudging to the pasture to get the cows for milking. Her husband didn't charge his mileage to the church when he went to see his Aunt Sophie in the hospital, so why should Willie? Why should Willie be reimbursed for hospital and house calls? That was his job, for Pete's sake! *Why should a minister be paid for doing his job?*

Once Missy's friends had gathered their incriminating evidence and crafted their impeccable logic to condemn Willie, there was still one last thing they felt conscience-bound to do. They had to rescue Missy from her life with that ax murderer, that sneak thief, that tax cheat, that imbecile, that good-for-nothing husband and drug runner Willie Goodenough.

Following the advice of the local psychiatrist Doc Fixyourbrain, Missy's friends decided on an intervention. Cornering Missy in her kitchen, they sat her down at the table, blocking all exits, doors and windows, and begged her to change her ways.

Tracy cried as she pleaded with Missy: "Missy, you know *we* love you and have your best interests at heart. We can't stand seeing you hurt and lonely like this. You need to dump that no-good husband of yours. He doesn't spend any time with you. He doesn't spend any money on you. He doesn't take you anywhere."

"Yes," Vicky chimed in. "He's worthless. Everybody says so. Nobody likes him. You'd be shocked at what people are saying about your husband. In the end, if you stay with him, people will reject you too!"

Then it was Lucy's turn: "Missy, I have just one question to ask you. When was the last time that bum, Willie, even opened a door for you?"

Missy thought for a while, and then she said, "Well, just yesterday, when I was carrying a case of beer, he grabbed the marshmallows, ran ahead, and opened the door for me. I thought that was pretty chivalrous. And just last week, on Valentine's Day, we did something really special. We took a truckload of garbage to the town dump, and he let me drive!"

Missy's friends almost fell off their chairs. Hour after hour the intervention went on, but without success. Everything they said went in one ear and out the other. It was as if they were talking to a weather-vane heifer sitting on top of a barn. The intervention failed miserably.

Then one day Missy's friends noticed that Willie's car was often parked near the same house in town, a house owned by an unmarried woman who was also a member of All Sports. Upon further investigation, they learned that Willie was always there at the same time and on the same day every week. Apparently Willie didn't want anyone to see him enter the house, because he looked every which way and waited for a moment when no one was there before he walked toward and into the woman's house. Very suspicious indeed!

As soon as those facts had been gathered, all three of Missy's friends once again descended on Missy to let her know about her husband's shenanigans. Their message was clear: "Missy, you can't be loyal to that no-good, rotten husband of yours, because he isn't loyal to you."

That night a heart-broken Missy was fixin' to question her no-good, rotten, and disloyal husband about his shenanigans when Willie beat her to the punch. "Hey, Missy! Happy birthday! Have I got a surprise for you." Willie went over to the piano and displayed his new skill. With one finger he haltingly played the Happy Birthday Song and serenaded her as he played.

"Honey, I've been taking piano lessons on the sly with our new member, Polly Plunkdakeys. I wanted to surprise you. I want to play for you and sing songs with you and spend more time with you. Maybe I can even learn to play hymns."

That was the good news. The next day came the bad news. Missy's friends, her best friends, her only real friends were all arrested or fined for some kind of misconduct. It was unbelievable. What are the chances of all of it happening on the same day?

Tracy Traitor, who had accused Willie of adding poison to his communion wine, was accused, along with her husband Perpa Traitor, of adding water to the milk they sold to the creamery. Tracy and her husband had to pay a $10,000 fine.

Vicky Vicious, who had reported that Willie was skimming money from the offerings, was arrested for skimming money from the bank where she worked. Later she'd be fined $30,000 and put on a year's probation.

Lucy Lipps, married to a farmer, was also in trouble with the law. It seems that she and her husband Tight Lipps had one hundred acres enrolled in the government's Conservation Reserve and Enhancement Program. They were being paid not to grow crops on that land, but somehow they forgot, and they grew and harvested crops on that 100 acres anyway. Now everyone was asking: *why should they be paid for not doing their job when they were doing their job?*

With her friends in trouble, Missy needed comfort and assurance from her husband. But Willie had no time for Missy. Three of his members were in trouble with the law. He had to comfort and counsel them. He had a couple dozen marriages breaking up in the congregation. He had a funeral on Friday. And, as if Pastor Goodenough didn't already have enough to do, just a couple of days earlier, at the last Church Council meeting, the church leaders asked Willie to make a time study, reporting how he used his time. *They were openly suggesting that Pastor Goodenough wasn't working hard enough.*

It was six weeks later when Willie and Missy finally had a chance to sit down and catch their breath. Missy said, "Willie, why do you suppose offerings suddenly went up when Judas Ananias passed away? With someone else counting the offerings the church has plenty of money now. I think there's a connection there."

"And Willie, about that time study for the Church Council, are you really going to hand one in? If you do, you should also report how many hours I spend helping you, answering the phone, typing the bulletins, being your secretary, and I don't get paid. Willie, these people are getting a real deal. They're getting two workers for the price of one. Yep, Willie, they're getting two for the price of one."

"Missy, let's not get our feathers in a heap! We'll get through this well enough. It's just another misunderstanding. The people here at All Sports have good hearts, Missy. The people here are our friends. They're wonderful friends, Missy!"

"Oh, Willie, I still say the harder a person works in the ministry the less people notice. *And the more you try to be a friend, the more people stay away.*"

Chapter Nineteen:
Funky Worship Wars

It was a dismal, rainy morning when Claude B. slumped into one of the chairs in Pastor Goodenough's office uninvited. Claude B. started out slowly and cautiously, "Pastor Willie, I've thought about this for a long time. I didn't wanna tell you, but I can't keep quiet anymore. And everybody in the congregation feels the same way. You wouldn't believe how many people have urged me to come to you, and some are your closest friends."

With that, Claude B. Critical paused to see what effect his words were having. *Nothing would have pleased him more than to see his pastor break out into a cold sweat or suddenly go into a table-thumping tremble or even to see Willie's teeth start to chatter in fear, then levitate and leave his body, hovering and clattering above his head.* But Pastor Goodenough remained his insanely positive and clueless self. In fact, he seemed eager to hear what Claude would say. Like a little boy about to hear what he was getting for his birthday, like a person deep in debt opening the mail and finding his tax refund, like an overheated hog sliding into the cooling depths of his favorite mud hole, Willie leaned forward expecting *good* news. "What is it, Claude?" Willie chirped, "What do you need to tell me?"

Obviously, what Claude was trying to do wasn't working. So it was time to lower the boom. *"Pastor Willie, I hate to tell you this, but worship here at All Sports is a lot like the weather today. It's dreary, dismal, and boring.* The hymns we sing aren't anything like the music people listen to on the radio. Your sermons are terrible, too. They're too long, not enough illustrations, too much Bible, too much about what Jesus did."

"Willie, what you're doing in the pulpit is like that old Chinese water torture with heavy drops of water pounding on peoples' foreheads. It's the same every week. Every Sunday you have the law and gospel chasin' one another around the church. First you've got the law bouncing off the walls, then the gospel, and then the law again. It's so predictable, Pastor, and so boring, and we can't stand it anymore."

"*A number of us have been visiting the Proselytin' Praise Palace, that new community church in Cadaver.* The worship there is exciting! The music is festive and upbeat. They've got a praise band, Willie, a whole orchestra leading the people in singing. And the pastor talks about us, what we should do, how we can be happy, not all this Bible stuff from hundreds of years ago! And that church is growing, Pastor!"

"Oh, and another thing, Pastor Willie, the reverend over there—his name is Barry Slick. He's so good looking! He's an Elvis look-alike, and he's such a smooth talker he makes the ladies swoon. My wife can't wait to go back. And they have this practice of hugging one another at the start of the service. The first time I went there I was sitting next to this really tall blond, and I got to hug her! It was wonderful!"

Claude B. Critical stopped for a moment to catch his breath, and then continued. "Pastor, here's how I feel, and all the others in this congregation as well: if we don't change, if we don't become a little more modern, a little more exciting, we're gonna die. We're gonna lose all our young people! *We need to adopt some of the methods successful churches are using to attract people or pretty soon, pastor, it's just you, your wife, and the organist attending here at All Sports.* There, I've said it. I didn't wanna say it. But the others made me say it. The whole congregation made me say it. Have a great day, Pastor!" And with that crushing burden taken off his shoulders and cast on Willie, Claude B. Critical walked out the door.

The next few days were a nightmare for Willie. One person after another paraded through his office adding fuel to the fire. He or she didn't want to come and tell Willie what to do. But the others made them do it. Everyone in the whole congregation—man and woman, young and old, rich and poor—were all united in their opinion that worship at All Sports had to change with the times, and if Willie didn't go along with what they wanted, he was toast. He was finished at All Sports.

Claude B. Critical and that whole crowd of complainers who paraded through Willie's office were quite convincing. Willie was absolutely sure that he was all alone. There was nobody on his side. Nobody. Willie and his liturgical way of worship were finished.

But, sure enough, at the next voters meeting it became clear that the congregation was hopelessly and evenly divided. *God be praised, there were actually two sides ready to fight to the death about this.* The one wanted change and more change, no matter what the cost. In their minds, it couldn't be wrong to follow the lead of growing churches. After all, wasn't growth the sign of God's approval? "Change or Die!" was the rallying cry for this group, as it championed ways to attract the curious.

The other side wanted to keep worship the same. They wanted it to be dignified, liturgical, and dedicated to teaching and nurturing God's children in the truth. The songs sung in worship weren't supposed to appeal to people's emotions. They were to increase people's knowledge. Worship wasn't supposed to be entertaining, but edifying!

The two sides were so evenly divided that it was impossible at first to pass any motions at the voters meeting that night. No matter what was proposed, the vote was always 12 to 12, and the chairman, Mickey "the Mouse" Edwards, alias "the Weasel," wouldn't break any of the ties, because, he said, he felt strongly both ways.

At the meeting, the two groups began chanting slogans at one another. "Change or die!" the one side shouted over and over again. "Remain in truth!" came from the others, as each side tried to drown out the other. The tension was so thick you couldn't see across the room. The tension was so thick Willie couldn't see anything past the floaters in his eyes. The tension was so thick that way down the hall the two bathroom fans recognized the problem, started up, and quickly shifted into overdrive. The tension was so great it tripped the smoke alarms.

Willie didn't know what to do. Mickey "the Mouse" Edwards, alias "the Weasel," didn't know what to do. The Church Council and the Elders didn't know what to do. The custodian and the church mice didn't know what to do. What future did All Sports have if these two evenly divided sides couldn't agree on anything?

Seeing the dilemma, but not knowing what to do, Pastor Willie briefly excused himself, telephoned Missy, and explained what was happening. Missy's solution came in an instant, and Willie brought it back to the voters.

So here's what they did. Sunday's worship was kept the way it had always been. And Monday night's worship became a predictable performance of "I love Jesus" lyrics set to country and western music.

And for a while everyone was happy. Sunday church-goers had what they were used to and the Monday crowd danced and sang to a brand new beat of heart-tugging tunes that rivaled anything the Proselytin' Praise Palace was doing across town. Even Willie welcomed some of the changes. He got a kick out of growing sideburns for the Monday night crowd, shortening his sermons, and filling them with cute little stories about his wife and family.

Yep! Everyone was happy as long as the two warring sides were kept apart. But All Sports still had to have quarterly voters meetings. And it was there that hostilities regularly broke out. "Change or die!" the one group chanted, the bathroom fans siding with them. "Remain in truth!" came the shout from the other side of the room, with the smoke alarms adding irritating decibels to their chant.

Then one day an immigrant from Afghanistan named Mohammed Allah Akhbar Mohammed and his wife came to All Sports. They took Willie's Bible Information Class, all sixteen lessons, and joined the church. Every weekend Mohammed and his wife attended services, both dressed in their traditional garb, Mohammed in his kufi (his hat) and his jellabiya (his cloak) and his wife in her hijab and burqa. And every weekend a whole train of followers tagged along behind them, all of them dressed in the same knee-and-ankle-covering duds. *It was wonderful!* Former Moslems and present Moslems hearing the Scriptures, singing hymns, and when they attended on Monday nights, dancing to "I love Jesus" lyrics set to country and western music.

But at the first voters meeting Mohammed attended, he demanded something that shook the very pillars of All Sports. He insisted that at every service Pastor Willie also read from the Koran. After all, that was a holy book, too, wasn't it? And if it was growth they wanted, why not read the Koran, like all those mosques were doing in the Middle East? No churches were growing as fast as they were, and nobody ever left the mosque!

Mohammed's suggestion would have been quickly voted down but for two reasons. One was the bulge that projected from his jellabiya right at his belt. Everyone knew how eager Jihadists were to carry out homicide bombings if they didn't get their way. Maybe that bulge was a suicide belt. How could they dare to make the Moslems angry? Willie thought that bulge at Mohammed's belt was probably the beer belly most middle-aged men had. But he didn't know for sure, and how could he take a chance?

The other thing that prompted a swift approval of Mohammed's demands were the dozen or so other Moslems who accompanied Mohammed to the meeting. They too had bulges at their belts under their jellabiyas. Were they suicide belts, .44 magnums, or beer bellies? Nobody knew, and no one, certainly not Mickey "the Mouse" Edwards, alias "the Weasel," was willing to take a chance.

All of Mohammed's proposals passed unanimously. And the next Sunday there were four readings: the Old Testament, the Epistle, the Gospel, and the Koran. When the Koran was read, the wives of both Christians and Moslems had to separate from their husbands and go to the back of the room. A significant part of the offering would now be siphoned off for the Taliban. A stained glass window was installed depicting Mohammed ascending into heaven, according to legend, at the Dome of the Rock. It was placed just opposite the window showing Jesus' ascension near Bethany. And, from that time on, at certain hours of the day, the Moslems would burst into the church, spread out their prayer rugs, kneel down, and pray toward the east.

Blended worship had come to All Sports Lutheran Church in its purest, most unadulterated, and most enlightened form. All Sports had surged ahead and leap-frogged everyone. And sure enough, worship services were packed every Sunday, standing room only. Spies came from the Proselytin' Praise Palace and from all over the world to see what new things All Sports was doing. There were people from near and far, from east and west, from heaven and hell. There were Parthians, Medes and Elamites, residents of Mesopotamia, Judea and Cappadocia, Pontus and Asia, Phrygia and Pamphylia, Egypt and the parts of Libya near Cyrene, visitors from Rome (both Christians and converts to Christianity); Cretans and Arabs. *They all came to see blended worship carried to its most extreme and insane limits.* The smell of success was in the air!

But unfortunately, this particular brand of success really didn't smell very good. All Sports Lutheran had become something its founders had never intended. The two sides that had been fighting funky worship wars suddenly realized that they were in over their heads. The change or die group realized that change wasn't always good. They actually yearned for the day when they could go back to the way it had always been.

It was woe-is-me time at All Sports. People were wringing their hands in despair. Even Mickey "the Mouse" Edwards was almost ready to take a stand. Pressure was building. District officials were demanding that something be done. Synod officials were asking what was going on. Willie was about to be defrocked. All Sports was about to be kicked out of the larger church body.

And then one day the Moslems just disappeared. One weekend none of them came to church. And the following week none of them came in to say their prayers. *They just disappeared and never came back. It was as if they had never existed.*

At the next voters meeting peace came to All Sports Lutheran Church. The two warring sides called a truce. There were no more shouting matches between "Change or die!" and "Remain in truth!" The smoke alarms and the bathroom fans once again maintained a holy silence. Worship was restored to what it had always been: dignified, liturgical and dedicated to teaching and nurturing God's children in the truth. Motions passed unanimously to get rid of the Koran, the Dome of the Rock stained glass window, the prayer rugs, the accordion, the drums, the fiddle, the horn that called the Moslems to prayer, and even Pastor Willie's sideburns. *The people at All Sports had learned a valuable lesson. Once again they would rely on God's Word for church growth rather than the latest innovations.*

That night, as Willie and Missy sat in their living room in front of the fireplace, Willie said, "I don't get it, Missy. Where did all those people go? How can so many people vanish off the face of the earth so quickly and thoroughly? And we had nothing to do with that!"

Missy took a deep breath and whispered softly, "Willie, it's not that we didn't do anything at all. I used my contacts with the CIA, and I arranged for Mohammed and his friends to hear that their relatives were in danger back in Afghanistan. Thank God they believed it! They all went back to Afghanistan. The CIA can deal with them a lot easier over there. They won't be back, Willie. My friends at the CIA have assured me of that."

"Oh, and one more thing, Willie. You know your good friend Claude B. Critical? I did some investigating, and I learned what his middle name is. It's Bumkin, Willie! Claude Bumkin Critical! *How could loving parents name their little boy Claude Bumkin?* No wonder he's been such a fault-finding, annoying schnook all his life. But I've talked to Claude, and I've persuaded him to change his middle name from

Bumkin to Barnabas. He won't bother you anymore, Willie. I've seen to that."

"That's great, Honey," Willie replied. "But I wish you could persuade Claude to change his last name too."

Right about then, Willie's eyelids began to droop, and his head started to bob. *Soon he was fast asleep, and Missy was left to her own, much weightier thoughts.*

Chapter Twenty:
Consternation Class

It was mid August. Willie had finally sat down to do his Confirmation planning for the school year. It was time to send a letter announcing when classes would begin and what the students should bring when they came.

With any luck, half the children would show up by the third week. People had learned from past experience that the pastor himself wouldn't be there any earlier. There was always some catastrophe that kept Willie from attending. His grandmother died ... again. His car ran out of gas. His pant leg got caught in a bear trap—and he couldn't walk out of the woods dressed in his underwear, could he? He and Father Janski got carried away discussing religious matters.

Those were some of the official explanations. The truth was that when classes were supposed to start, Missy usually found Willie hiding somewhere: in the furnace room, in the church basement, in the neighbor's pole shed behind the lawnmower, in a boxcar headed for Auschwitz, Indiana. Once she found him cowering in the fetal position in a tree. Willie hated Confirmation class even more than the kids did.

But who could blame him? Most of the kids Willie had in class couldn't read or write. They were in special education at school. Some were borderline autistic. Some were bipolar and constantly fighting.

This year one of them was twenty-two years old. His name was Herman Dumkopf. All Sports was the third church and Willie the fourth pastor charged with teaching him something about God and the Bible. It was hopeless. Herman stuttered profusely. He had been through three years of speech therapy, but the problem was his speech therapist was an unconverted stutterer. Beyond his p-p-p-persistent speech impediment, Herman had far deeper deficiencies. Whenever Willie asked him who the Trinity was, he would say, "M-m-m-mo, C-c-c-curly, and L-l-l-larry!" The Bible was written by L-l-l-luther and the catechism was written by G-g-g-god. The Lord's Supper was for p-p-people who couldn't w-w-wait to get home for l-l-l-lunch.

The one girl in Confirmation class this year was pregnant. Willie was pretty sure this wouldn't be a virgin birth, because the young man responsible wasn't named Joseph and her name wasn't Mary.

Having a pregnant fourteen-year-old in the class presented a challenge. The question wasn't whether Willie should confirm her but whether he should also secretly confirm the baby. Secretly confirming the baby years before it entered Confirmation class could give Willie a victory of sorts. Years later, when her parents pulled her out of Confirmation class, angry with Willie for some silly reason, Willie could say, "It's too late! I've already confirmed her!" That would fix their little red Subaru.

As Willie agonized over the coming year, his thoughts turned to the trouble he had the previous year picking a Sunday for Confirmation. That year May had only four Sundays. The first Sunday was the opening of the sport fishing season in Wisconsin, a religious festival rivaling Easter in importance. If Willie scheduled Confirmation on that day, there'd be threats on his life.

The last Sunday was Memorial Day Weekend, when everybody left town. The third Sunday was the Day of the Dead in Cadaver. The Day of the Dead was the brain child of the business community, which was desperately trying to build up tourism. Other towns had festivals. There were hamburger festivals, brat festivals, cranberry festivals, apple festivals, zucchini, pumpkin and potato festivals. There were maple syrup festivals, harvest festivals, beef liver festivals, October festivals, and even square dance festivals. All of them, of course, were really beer festivals, but they were given different names for the sake of variety.

For years, the town of Cadaver didn't have a festival, but the town fathers fixed that by instituting the Day of the Dead on the third Sunday of May. Cadaver, you'll remember, had three important businesses dedicated to the thriving death industry. Some years before, all three had suddenly closed. But, like Lazarus come back from the dead, they all had since reopened. With new owners and more modern plants, each was even more successful than before. One plant made caskets. Another made headstones. And a third manufactured grave diggers. What could be more appropriate than having a day to honor these wonderful businesses, a special day to celebrate the fact that dying people were once again keeping Cadaver alive?

Everybody in town dressed up like zombies, goons, mummies, or skeletons. Even the churches had a special role to play in the festival. They had mock funerals as a part of the celebration. If there was a real funeral and somebody actually died, so much the better!

While the churches were holding mock funerals, most of the adults gathered around the beer tents drinking red beer, dyed to look like blood. The children were busy bobbing for body parts, or they lined up for skull bowling, or they pinned the tail on the Grim Reaper. There were prizes for those who got the closest in guessing the weight of the next corpse brought to the Slabum and Plantemdeep Mortuary.

So it really wasn't a hard decision last year when to schedule Confirmation. The first Sunday was the opening of fishing. The third Sunday was the Day of the Dead. And the last Sunday landed on Memorial Day weekend. The only Sunday left was the second Sunday, which was Mothers Day, *but it was a perfect fit!* Families would want to gather anyway on Mothers Day, wouldn't they? What could be better than to have mothers and grandmothers—yes, the whole family— gathered around, congratulating and encouraging the confirmands in their faith?

Willie was completely taken by surprise three weeks before Confirmation when a group of women from the congregation suddenly descended on his office. They were weeping uncontrollably and gnashing their teeth. When one of them finally calmed down enough to talk, the words came fast and furiously. "Pastor Willie, how could you do this? You've ruined our day! You've stolen our one special day, Mother's Day, and made it Confirmation Day. It was all we had, and now we have nothing. We always knew you hated women, and now we know for sure!" Nothing Willie said in his defense made any difference. He had ruined Mother's Day!

This year, thankfully, there were five Sundays in the month of May. Maybe Willie could schedule Confirmation on the fourth Sunday. But then Willie remembered something recently published in the Cadaver Deadtree Post. The high school had announced that two kids might actually graduate this year. This was an unprecedented development! *If it happened, these would be the first graduates from Cadaver High for two decades!*

If there was a graduation at Cadaver High, Willie couldn't have Confirmation on the same day. That would be stealing thunder from the high school and from those two special kids who should be celebrated more enthusiastically than heroes come back from war.

Nobody ever graduated from Cadaver High! Normally, the girls attended until they got pregnant. And then two or three boys would immediately leave town. The standard practice was to enter high school, stay as long as you could, and then drop out and go for your GED. But for the people in Cadaver, even that was difficult. After numerous attempts, Herman's father, Immer Dumkopf, finally got his GED just weeks before his first Social Security check. The nursing homes in Cadaver were filled with people refusing to die until all their kids finally had their GEDs. If there was a graduation at Cadaver High School, a precious and unprecedented graduation on the fourth Sunday of May, there was no way Willie could possibly have Confirmation that day!

So, all things considered, this year it would be an easy choice for Willie. In fact, it was a shoo-in. *Willie triumphantly scheduled Confirmation for the fourth Sunday of May.* With the high school planning graduation on that Sunday, Willie knew the day would be free. It was like golf. If you aimed for the tree, you wouldn't hit it. If you took your umbrella to the park, it wouldn't rain. If you took toilet paper along with you in the boat, you wouldn't need it. And if Cadaver High School scheduled a graduation, you could be sure there wouldn't be one.

Once more Willie thought about the young people he was expecting in Confirmation class this year. There were nine boys, one twenty-two-year-old Dumkopf, and one pregnant girl. Not a lot of balance to the group. Willie looked at the list and instinctively knew that this year more than ever he would need the skills of an animal trainer at the circus.

Kids that age sometimes smelled like animals, like denned up bears or wet dogs. There would be twenty-four smelly arm pits, including Willie's, in a room designed by an architect to hold twelve! There weren't nearly enough windows. Willie gasped just thinking about it and made a mental note to ask the Building and Grounds Committee to knock out an outside wall.

At that moment the phone rang. It was Mrs. Dumkopf. "Pastor Willie, I know Confirmation class will be starting soon, and I called to say that I hope that Herman will be confirmed this year. Pastor, I know he can learn. We did finally get him potty-trained, you know. And he learned to tie his shoes. He even learned the alphabet last year, and he counts to 666. He's not hopeless, Pastor Willie. I know you can teach him something about God, even though we never could."

"This summer we got him a Ouija board for his birthday. We taught him all about the devil, and that he learned real quick. And since that time his voice has changed."

"What do you mean his voice has changed?"

"Well, it's deeper now and kind of gravelly. It really doesn't sound much like Herman anymore. He makes a lot of threats, and he curses a lot. Anyway, we'll bring him to Confirmation class real regular, and if he's confirmed this year, there's a slaughtered hog in it for ya. Thanks, Pastor, for all your hard work!" With that, Lena Dumkopf hung up the phone.

For the next ten minutes Willie tried to decide whether he should have the exorcism before, after, or at the same time as the confirmation. Having it on the same day, as a kind of package deal, maybe he'd get more than a slaughtered hog out of the Dumkopfs. But, of course, the last thing he'd want was a hog in his freezer that was possessed by the devil! Willie loved deviled eggs, but he'd never tasted deviled pork.

Willie quickly finished his letter to the parents announcing the start of Confirmation class. Then he ran off the form he used to collect personal information from the kids, things like their names, their parents' names, their places of birth. Those were things he needed for the church records later on. Unfortunately, there was always a kid who couldn't spell his name, or didn't know his middle name. And most of them wouldn't know who their father was.

"Aren't you done with that letter yet?" It was the voice of his beloved wife Missy. He had promised to do some things with her that day, and she was becoming a little impatient.

"Are you daydreaming in there, or what? Gitter done!"

Missy had every right to be a little impatient. The letter Willie was preparing should have been sent out a week ago. But every year it was more difficult to do it. Every year Willie dreaded Confirmation class more and more. It wasn't Confirmation class anymore. It was Consternation class.

Willie had to find a better place to hide this year. Missy always found him! Where could he hide? Maybe he could tie himself to the ceiling fan in the church. Nobody would look for him there. But wouldn't he get a little dizzy up there, going round and round? Maybe he could hide in the church dumpster or go down to the Styx River, slide under the water and breathe through a straw!

"Wait a minute," Willie said to himself. "How many years do I have left if I retire at sixty-five? Let's see. Twenty-five years … five months … and … eleven days. Hey, Missy! Guess what! I just thought of something!"

The countdown had begun. And Willie hadn't even left his office that morning! *From that time on, Willie realized how advantageous it was, in the midst of trouble, to have something wonderful to look forward to. That's probably why God told us about heaven.*

Chapter Twenty-One:
Squeaky Clean

Squeak! *Squeeeeeeeak*! There it was again! All Willie had to do was shift his weight to one side or another in his office chair, and that maddening squeak would blow the wax right out of his ears. It was so loud it drowned out the noon whistle blasting out of city hall. It was so loud that one year Willie never heard the fire works on the fourth of July.

Willie had tried to fix the squeak. He had slathered the bottom half of that chair with motor oil applied with a dripping paint brush. He had tried diesel oil, machine oil, bath oil, fish oil, vegetable oil, corn oil, canola oil, olive oil, peanut oil, sun tan oil, and leftover Communion wine. Nothing had any effect on that fog-horn squeak.

There was one magic day some years ago when that annoying squeak was mysteriously absent. That day Willie had shifted his weight back and forth, and the chair didn't squeak! That was the good news. The bad news was that on that day everything else squeaked. The office door squeaked. The office window squeaked when it was opened. Every drawer of Willie's desk squeaked. Willie's pen squeaked when it touched paper. That day the noon whistle didn't blow, it squeaked. And that same day Willie's telephone didn't ring with its usual tone. It squeaked when a call was coming in.

The easy solution for a squeaky chair was to get a new one. But every time Willie requested a new chair from the Building and Grounds Committee, his request was denied. *When he tried to show the committee how annoying the squeak was, the chair wouldn't squeak. It* was as if that chair had a brain. It knew that if it squeaked in the presence of a committee member it would be gone.

All things considered, of course, that squeaky chair was actually a minor inconvenience compared to all the maddening annoyances, dilemmas, and cans of worms that Willie had been dealing with lately, all of them connected with his job.

There were terrified women who came to Willie's door in the wee hours of the morning, looking for sanctuary and hoping to escape a beating from their drunken husbands. Missy would put them up in the guest bedroom or let them sleep on the couch.

Sometimes the husbands of these same women would come to Willie's door moments later asking to be let into church. They might claim, for example, that they wanted to get into church to find their glasses, but even Willie could see that they were actually wearing their glasses. Or they would say they had forgotten to give their offering last Sunday and they wanted to drop it off before they spent it. But even Willie knew this couldn't be true. Their real reason to enter the church, of course, was to find their wives, or maybe, if they were lucky, find communion wine in the cupboard or beer money in the mission offering box.

"Willie!" Missy said to him one day, "You're going to have to get a gun to protect yourself. *One of these days all these kindnesses of yours will come down on your head like a load of chicken manure dumped on a rat.* It's all going to backfire like the time you co-signed that loan for old Sammy Snakeoil. I still can't understand how you could co-sign a loan for someone 102 years old claiming he was going to start a business! You had to know you'd soon be holding the bag on that one! Willie, you need to get a gun. You need a backbone. And you have to learn to say 'No!'"

Even worse than the drunks that were disturbing the peace at All Sports was the unrelenting faultfinding, the snide remarks about his sermons, the crude reminders of the time, years ago, that he mispronounced a word, or the time he forgot someone's name or dropped a communion wafer. *Was Willie the only person in the world who wasn't perfect?*

Was it only Willie's imagination, or did Sneaky Pete Peterson really stick out his foot to trip Willie in the hall? Was he dreaming, or did old Granny Gladiator run her car head-on into his on purpose? Why was his car the only one that got nasty dents and scratches from the shopping carts in the grocery store parking lot? Why was his house the only one toilet-papered on homecoming? Did that skunk actually die on his front lawn last week or was it placed there?

Willie's sufferings were considerable. Five times he had received from the Voters Meeting the forty lashes minus one. Three times he was beaten with rods. Once he was stoned and wanted no one to know about it. Three times he was car-wrecked. He had spent a night and a day in a disabled canoe. He had labored and toiled and gone without sleep. He had known hunger and thirst when his money didn't stretch till payday. He had been cold and naked stepping out of his shower. And he had faced daily the pressure of his concern for All Sports.

Just when Willie thought that he couldn't take any more, the squeak problems got worse. Everything around Willie began to squeak. Willie's comb squeaked when he ran it through his hair. The buttons on his TV remote squeaked. The books in his library squeaked. His computer squeaked. The smoke going up his chimney squeaked. Everything he touched, everything he looked at, and everything he was close to squeaked.

"Missy! I'm going nuts! Everything squeaks, and I don't know what causes it. What should I do?"

Without any hesitation, Missy said, "Willie, I think it's time for Squeakbusters."

"How do I get hold of them?" Willis asked.

"The number's in the phone book. Look it up." And with that, Missy ran to take something that was squeaking out of the oven.

Two days later, a short, stout woman, wearing Coke-bottle glasses, appeared at the door. It was Toni Tonerdown from Squeakbusters. She announced that undercover Squeakbuster trucks and vans were already patrolling the streets of Cadaver with hyper-sensitive electronic equipment, and she was confident that within hours they would uncover the source of all the devilish squeaks that were troubling Willie. She also assured Willie that none of this would cost him anything. Squeakbuster expenses were covered by government grants through the Environmental Protection Agency. *When Willie invited her in for coffee, she politely declined, saying that for her own safety and sanity there was no way she would enter a house emitting so many loud squeaks.*

By the next day, the squeaking had stopped. Willie's chair no longer squeaked. His comb didn't squeak. The buttons on his remote didn't squeak. The books in his library didn't squeak. The smoke going up his chimney didn't squeak. Even the church mice had stopped squeaking. It was a new normal, one that Willie had been hoping for but never thought he would experience in his lifetime.

Then, a couple of hours after the squeaking stopped, Toni Tonerdown appeared at the door and asked to come in. While sipping a cup of coffee, she began to disclose what Squeakbusters had found.

"This was quite an unusual case," she said, "and quite sophisticated. It seems that not all the people in your congregation like you, Pastor Goodenough. To make you feel a little better, that is not unusual, Pastor. *Most of the cases Squeakbusters deals with have pastors, priests, and rabbis as their victims."*

"But the thing that made this case unusual was the equipment used and the number of people in on the scheme. At this time we have three couples under indictment for unauthorized squeak production. These same individuals are also charged with producing illegal squeak-emitting machines and selling them to clergy-haters all around the Midwest."

"All six are members of your church. One is your secretary Ima Quisling and her husband. Another, a man named Fred Fixitnot, claims to be the head of the Building and Grounds Committee here at All Sports. The third is a fellow named Ned Needadrink. He's one of the town drunks and has been jailed numerous times for beating his wife. As you probably realize, all these people have had access to your house and the church buildings, at which time they installed their equipment. They controlled the equipment from master panels in their homes. It really was quite a sophisticated operation, but if we've got all the culprits, and we think we have, you shouldn't have any more problems. *The air waves in this town are now squeaky clean!"*

With that, Toni Tonerdown handed Willie a pile of government forms to sign, certifying that Squeakbusters had done its job. He signed and dated everything, and then she was gone. That left Willie and Missy sitting alone in that numbing quiet around the kitchen table.

Willie was the first to speak. "Missy, I don't understand how something like this can happen. You know how much I love the people here. Every year I fight for a raise for my secretary. Sometimes she gets a raise and I don't. And then she repays me like this! And think of all the things around All Sports that need fixing or painting, and I do the work myself. I try not to ask Fred Fixitnot to fix anything. I know he's busy.

And this is how he repays me! And how many times didn't we shelter Ned Needadrink's wife so she wouldn't get a beating, and we never called the police! And this is how that family repays us! I just don't understand!"

"Willie, I told you that one day all these kindnesses of yours would come down on your head like a load of chicken manure dumped on a rat. I told you it was all going to backfire like the time you co-signed for old Sammy Snakeoil. *A lot of these people are like porcupines, Willie. You get too close to them, and you're going to get hurt.*"

"Willie, don't feel so bad that not everybody at All Sports likes you. *The problem is, they don't love the Lord.* They hate *Him*, Willie! But because they can't walk right up to God and poke a finger in *His* eye, they do it to you."

"They don't like God's Commandments either, Willie. They hate you, because you remind them of God's Commandments. *And it's all about control, Willie.* They want All Sports to be *their* church, not *God's* church, and you stand in the way. That's why they hate you, Willie. That's why they hate you. *But you just keep preaching God's love and you keep loving your people, and everything will turn out okay.*"

Willie listened to all of this very intently, he sighed deeply, and then, as he walked out the door, Missy heard him mumbling to himself: "Nineteen years, two months, and twelve days."

Chapter Twenty-Two:
Kid Trouble

The sound of the telephone ringing on the nightstand brought Willie out of a deep sleep. He glanced at the clock. It was two o'clock in the morning. This wasn't good.

The telephone rang again. Who could it be? Did somebody in the congregation die or have an accident? Did some hobo need money to get to the next town? Did someone desperately need a copy of last Sunday's sermon? Was it someone so anxious to give a guilt offering to the church that he couldn't wait till morning? Shaking the cobwebs out of his brain, Willie realized that the only way to find out who was calling was to answer the phone.

"Hello, Pastor Goodenough here!"

"Pastor Goodenough, I hate to bother you at this late hour, but this is Sergeant Weave Gotcha with the Cadaver Police Department. We have a young lady down here at the station who says she's your daughter. We have her name as Queen B. Goodenough.

Reverend, we picked her up for being drunk and disorderly. When we brought her down to the station, we had to put her in the lock-up, because she wouldn't settle down. She kept screaming and trying to kick our officers in the shins. Reverend, if this is your daughter, we'd like you to come down here and take her home as soon as you can before she puts one of my officers in the hospital or trashes my station."

"Okay, officer, I'll be there in a few minutes!"

Willie hung up the phone and reluctantly told Missy what he had just heard from Sergeant Gotcha. They quickly dressed and hurried to the police station, dreading what they would find. It was pretty quiet in the car. The shame and disappointment were overwhelming.

How could their daughter turn out like this? Why was she always acting up? Their son Kenny B. Goodenough seemed to be growing up to be an orderly and productive citizen. Why couldn't his sister settle down? And what would the congregation say if they heard about this? The pastor's daughter arrested for being drunk and disorderly! What if this was reported in the newspaper?

When Willie and Missy arrived at the police station, they were surprised to hear loud music coming from inside. There were sounds of uproarious laughter and squeals of delight. When they entered the station, they found their daughter Queen B. dancing to the Beer Barrel Polka with Sergeant Gotcha. Two other officers were sitting in the room clapping and stomping their feet to the sound of the music. It was obvious that everyone was having a good time.

When the music stopped, Sergeant Gotcha noticed that Willie and Missy had arrived. "Reverend! Mrs. Goodenough! How are you this fine morning?"

Willie was about to give the usual speech that he always used to apologize for his daughter, but the sergeant kept talking. "So glad you're here to pick up your daughter. Enough of this dancing! We have to get back to work. There won't be any charges, Reverend. Queen B. has explained to our satisfaction what set her off down at Whiskey Bill's. They had no right to water down her beer. We sympathize with your daughter completely. You just take your lovely daughter home. Get her outta here. You have a wonderful daughter there, Reverend."

Willie was stunned, but he shouldn't have been. Queen B. was an expert at manipulating people. She could wrap the most unwilling subject around her little finger at a moment's notice. She could charm the leaves off a tree. She could melt the ice on a winter sidewalk. She could make crocodiles laugh and hyenas cry. She could make a flock of geese going south do a U-turn and fly north. Queen B. had maneuvered her way out of trouble more times than anyone could count.

What were Willie and Missy going to do with their daughter? It wouldn't do any good to take Queen B. back to the town psychiatrist, Doc Fixyourbrain. Last time they did that, Queen B. convinced the good doctor that she was fine but the rest of the family needed help. She almost succeeded in getting her parents committed to the county asylum!

Willie couldn't forget the time Queen B. got caught at the high school with peppermint schnapps in her locker. Somehow she convinced the principal that the peppermint schnapps had been prescribed by her doctor. One time she attended somebody's birthday party a few miles away, got drunk, and then got lost. Too brain dead to think clearly, she stopped and asked a policeman how to get home. He promptly took her to jail. That was another late night, another unplanned trip to a police station for her proud parents!

Then there was the brand new black leather jacket that Queen B. brought home one day. Where did she get the money? Was it stolen? And why was she always asking if she could paint her room black? Had she joined some satanic cult or witches coven? And what about the two little dolls she kept in her room that looked suspiciously like her parents? Those dolls had dozens of needles stuck in them. Was Queen B. practicing voo-doo?

A lot of people tried to help Willie and Missy, anonymously, of course. There were numerous unsigned letters that came in the mail. Each one reported some new and shameful misdeed by Queen B. People saw her being drunk and disorderly. She was skinny-dipping in a neighbor's pool. She had stolen apples from a neighbor and kicked his cat. She was rumored to be shoplifting. She was seen participating in a fist fight and hair-pull. She had joined a gang. She had robbed a bank. She was growing marijuana in a public drainage ditch. Someone saw her walking around downtown draped in a Nazi flag.

All of the letters quoted Bible passages, such as the one Paul wrote to Timothy: "Now an overseer ... must manage his own family well and see that his children obey him with proper respect. If anyone does not know how to manage his own family, how can he take care of God's church?" (1 Timothy 3:2–5) Even the full weight of Solomon's wisdom was tossed at the beleaguered parents: "He who spares the rod hates his child." (Proverbs 13:24)

Then one day Willie was sitting in his office trying to get some work done, and three men suddenly appeared in the doorway. It was the church elders. James the Elder came in first, followed by John the Elder, and, sure enough, the last one through the door was Pliny the Elder.

"Reverend, we came to talk to you about your daughter. She's out of control. Her behavior has the whole town talking. All Sports can't tolerate this kind of scandal. We had a meeting last night at the Last

Nail in the Coffin Bar and Grill. We decided that you can no longer be our pastor, and it takes effect today. Reverend Hooligan, over in Comatosa, has agreed to be the vacancy pastor. You have until tomorrow to empty out your office and retrieve any personal items you might have. Sorry, Pastor, but that's the way it is. The voters have spoken, and it was unanimous."

Bang! Crash! The wonderful sound of broken glass mercifully woke Willie out of a deep sleep as Missy accidentally knocked a lamp to the floor in the bedroom. The broken lamp was the answer to Willie's prayers! It was a dream! It was only a nightmare! Queen B. hadn't been misbehaving! Willie hadn't been kicked out of All Sports. It was all a dream! It was only a nightmare! Wow! That was a close call!

In the fog of waking up, Willie realized that he would have to take this dream seriously. It was like a shot across his bow. From now on, he would have to do things much differently as a parent. From now on, he'd have to discipline his children the way they should be disciplined!

"Wait a minute." Willie thought to himself. "We don't have any kids yet, do we?"

"Willie! Willie! Wake up, Willie! We've got a big day ahead of us. This is call day, Willie! You've got to wake up and get ready to go to the seminary. Today we find out where the Lord is going to send us! I sure hope it's a nice place, Willie. I hope it's a nice place. You know what I mean. *Like the kind of places we've been dreamin' about.*"

About the Author

Pastor Lyle L. Luchterhand entered the parish ministry in 1970. He holds a Master of Sacred Theology degree from Wisconsin Lutheran Seminary in Mequon, Wisconsin, and has served congregations in both Illinois and Wisconsin. Aside from the present volume of humorous fiction, Pastor Luchterhand has published several works of serious theology: *Man: From Glory to Ashes and Back* (1998); *The Lord's Anointed: Advent and Christmas Devotions for Young and Old* (2009); *His Hand among the Nations: Seeing God's Control in the Old Testament World* (2013); and *Joseph: Forgiving Brother* (2015). He and his wife of fifty-two years, Jean, have raised two sons (both now in the ministry) and two daughters.

Mothering Many: Sanity-Saving Strategies from Moms of Four or More, by Marie K. MacPherson.

25 moms of 160+ children navigate 56 challenges that mothers frequently face: menu-planning, laundry, time-management, self-care, homeschooling, intimacy, home-devotions, and much more!

Conceived by one perplexed mom and gestated over eight years, *Mothering Many* has finally been birthed through a labor of love by dozens of fellow Christian women. Literally written between nursing babies and wiping bottoms, this book offers hundreds of strategies, insights, and ideas for strengthening your home for the Lord. So, if you're too busy from the rigors of motherhood to brainstorm for improvement, crack open this book and let these moms troubleshoot for you!

Bonus sections of this book include: a comparison between the editor's own perspective as a mother of three in 2010 and a mother of five in 2016; a quiz for discovering your own mothering personality; plus insights from seven "mature moms" whose children are now grown and raising children of their own. Discussion questions are provided for use in moms' groups.

Debating Evolution before Darwinism: An Exploration of Science and Religion in America, 1844–1859, by Ryan C. MacPherson, Ph.D.

Fifteen years before Darwin's *Origin of Species* shook the world, a debate over evolution already raged in America's classrooms, churches, and scientific institutions. *Vestiges of Creation*, published anonymously by the Scottish journalist Robert Chambers in 1844, boldly marshaled recent scientific discoveries into a sweeping hypothesis of naturalistic development. Crafting a narrative energetic enough for lay readers, but supported with footnotes thorough enough for scholars, Dr. MacPherson reveals unexpected interactions between religion and science during this crucial era.

www.intoyourhandsllc.com/publishing/books

Also Published by Into Your Hands LLC

"Church Control or Birth Control": Margaret Sanger's Propaganda Campaign against the Catholic Church, by Nicholas Kaminsky, M.A.

The name Margaret Sanger is nearly synonymous with birth control in the United States. A controversial character even now, she founded the predecessor to today's Planned Parenthood and dedicated her life to working tirelessly for the legalization and promotion of birth control and abortion. While scholars have directed some attention toward Sanger's provocative statements on race and ethnicity, few have documented her vehement anti-Catholicism or shown the way she cleverly used anti-Catholic propaganda to promote her birth control crusade. Kaminsky has now done so. In this book, he demonstrates the way in which Sanger exploited powerful anti-Catholic sentiment in the United States to portray her fight for birth control as a struggle for American Freedom against a moral domination by the Catholic Church.

Rediscovering the American Republic, Volume 1: 1492-1877 and *Volume 2: 1877–Present*, by Ryan C. MacPherson, Ph.D.

Each volume contains over 700 pages of time-tested teaching tools, collectively spanning ten major epochs of American history: Pre-Columbian to British North America, 1492–1763; The Creation of the American Republic, 1763–1789; The Power of Political Parties, 1789–1836; Liberty, Slavery, and American Destiny, 1836–1860; The Civil War and Reconstruction, 1860–1877; America in the Gilded Age, 1877–1901; Progressive Reform and Human Nature, 1901–1929; The Emergence of the American Superpower, 1929–1953; The Cold War and Civil Rights, 1953–1981; The Triumph and the Vulnerability of the World's Only Superpower, 1981–Present.

www.intoyourhandsllc.com/publishing/books

Coming Soon!

Lessons Learned at Home:
Families Tell Their Homeschooling Stories

Christian home educators offer a unique perspective in today's complicated world of opportunities and decisions. The families represented in this book share their experiences and answer significant questions, including:

- ♥ *Why* do some families educate their children primarily in the home, others utilize public or parochial schools, and still others try some of each?

- ♥ *How* do Progressive, Classical, Christian, and Unschooling models for education differ from each other, and is it possible to integrate these philosophies into a coherent approach?

- ♥ *What* distinctive emphases do Lutheran, Catholic, and Reformed home education resources offer families?

- ♥ *How* do home educating parents coordinate their family schedules, select curricula, and track their progress?

- ♥ *What* have home educators done to pass muster with state requirements, make use of taxpayer-funded services, and prepare their children for the "real world"?

- ♥ *How* can home educators constructively address the concerns of grandparents, pastors, neighbors or others who have doubts about children not being in school?

- ♥ *Where* should you turn for more information, without wasting your time in the vast sea of online resources?

Whether you currently home educate your children, would like to do so, or are afraid to try, this book provides the insights you need to make an informed judgment—and to explain your choices to those who think differently.

To volunteer to participate in our homeschool family survey, or to order this book, visit:

www.intoyourhandsllc.com/publishing/books/71a